S0-COP-246

"Problems?" Dake whispered.

Melissa fought to keep her balance on undependable legs. Finally she nodded. "I find you very attractive," she said softly. Her eyes remained on the floor, but she sensed that he was smiling.

"Clearly the feeling is mutual," he said. "Go on."

She took a deep breath. The air was easily identifiable: the air of a hotel room in the middle of the night.

"This is *not* what I came here for," she said more firmly.

Dake tucked a finger under her chin and raised her face until she was looking directly at him. "Then why did you come, Mel?"

Other Second Chance at Love books by
Sarah Crewe

GOLDEN ILLUSIONS   #135
NIGHT FLAME   #195
SEAFLAME   #233

Sarah Crewe, who currently makes her home with her husband and two daughters in a small Pennsylvania town, has almost always lived in big cities, both in the United States and abroad. Among these was Chicago, the setting for Windflame and a city close to her heart. Due to her past volunteer work for VISTA, her studies for advanced degrees, and her professor husband's research, she has enjoyed a number of travel experiences, including several European ventures (one of her daughters celebrated her first birthday in Rome!) and forays into Africa and the Middle East. A theater and movie lover, Sarah says she has always been an avid reader and writer, and that her husband is always "my primary critic and editor."

Dear Reader:

The August books are here—and what a terrific bunch they are!

In *Such Rough Splendor* (#280), Cinda Richards—who delighted us with her zany *This Side of Paradise* (#237)—has penned a romance that we think will become a classic of the genre. The best elements of romance come together with superlative skill in this warm, funny, poignant tale of love and healing, as divorcée Amelia Taylor makes war and peace with, in her words, "the biggest, dumbest cow puncher she's ever clapped eyes on." Houston "Mac" McDade will live on in your memories as one of the most original and irresistible heroes you've ever had the good fortune to lock horns with!

Sarah Crewe explores the complexities of pursuit and revenge in *Windflame* (#281), a strong follow-up to her earlier romances. Melissa Markham's job as college fundraiser forces her to pursue wealthy Dakin Quarry for his money, but her immediate attraction to him vastly complicates the situation. Distrust, scandal, revenge, and Dakin's own fatal passion for Melissa combine to form a compelling, tension-filled love story set against a quiet college campus.

Lauren Fox's zest-filled, lusty romance *Storm and Starlight* (#282) will catch you up and whirl you away—just as Eric Nielson does to Maggie McGuire when she arrives to investigate the proposed expansion of his satellite-dish manufacturing company. There's never a dull moment as Maggie struggles to curb Eric's exuberant excesses and Eric gets Maggie into one outrageous situation after another. The banter flies fast and furious and the action's nonstop as these two forceful characters love and live with passionate energy.

In *Heart of the Hunter* (#283), Liz Grady has outdone herself, creating Mitch Cutter, a hard-boiled, gun-slinging bounty hunter who fears nothing except love, and Leigh Bramwell, a dyed-in-the-wool romantic with a long streak of cowardice. Never has a man so inept with "nice girls"—a man whose only way of loving a woman is by deceiving and possessing her—seemed so heart-wrenchingly appealing. *Heart of the Hunter* is a romance you'll read with excitement—and cherish for years to come.

Lucky's Woman (#284) will tug at your heartstrings and make you smile through your tears as only a romance by Delaney Devers can. With roughhewn "Lucky" Verret and ladylike Summer Jordan, Delaney creates a love so potent it has the power to destroy the very hearts it fills. You'll shiver with Summer as she braves mosquitoes, mud-creatures, and mayhem in the Louisiana swamp she loathes, in order to prove her loyalty to stubborn-as-sin Lucky. You'll ache with Lucky as he hides his longing from the woman he secretly cherishes but fears he cannot trust. All of you who raved about Delaney's *The Heart Victorious* (TO HAVE AND TO HOLD #40) and asked for more will find *Lucky's Woman* just the treat you've been waiting for.

Finally, SECOND CHANCE AT LOVE is pleased and proud to introduce a stunning new talent—Elizabeth N. Kary, author of *Portrait of a Lady* (#285). Here is an adult romance in the best sense of the word, the story of two complex characters whose struggles to trust and understand each other lead to an intimacy that's deep and powerfully satisfying. The maturity of Elizabeth's characters, the elegance of her writing style, and the page-turning quality of her story all set *Portrait of a Lady* apart as truly special. Don't miss the debut of this wonderful writer—and don't miss her first historical romance, *Love, Honor and Betray,* to be published by Berkley in January. This epic adventure and passionate love story set during the War of 1812 is destined to establish Elizabeth N. Kary as a romance writer of stature!

Enjoy these August romances and please keep your letters and questionnaires coming. We love reading them.

Best,

Ellen Edwards

Ellen Edwards, Senior Editor
SECOND CHANCE AT LOVE
The Berkley Publishing Group
200 Madison Avenue
New York, NY 10016

WINDFLAME

SARAH CREWE

SECOND CHANCE AT LOVE
BOOK

WINDFLAME

Copyright © 1985 by Sarah Crewe

All rights reserved. No part of this publication may be reproduced or transmitted in any form or by any means, electronic or mechanical, including photocopy, recording, or any information storage and retrieval system, without permission in writing from the publisher.

Requests for permission to make copies of any part of the work should be mailed to: Permissions, Second Chance at Love, The Berkley Publishing Group, 200 Madison Avenue, New York, NY 10016.

First edition published August 1985

First printing

"Second Chance at Love" and the butterfly emblem are trademarks belonging to Jove Publications, Inc.

Printed in the United States of America

Second Chance at Love books are published by
The Berkley Publishing Group
200 Madison Avenue, New York, NY 10016

For my father,
who taught me about track and field,
and many other things

WINDFLAME

- 1 -

MELISSA MARKHAM SLAMMED the car door shut and hurried up the stairs from the underground parking lot to the back entrance of the Art Institute of Chicago. A warm September breeze off Lake Michigan touched her face as she emerged briefly into the open air.

"I have an appointment at the Terrace Café," she called to a guard at the double glass doors. The short line of people buying admission tickets to the museum proper parted for her, and, rather than wait for an elevator, she took the stairs down to the restaurant two at a time.

The restaurant wasn't open yet. In the sculpture gallery that served as its entrance hall, a man in jeans and a tweed jacket stood alone, one hand jammed in his back pocket. He was checking the watch on his other wrist. Melissa came to an abrupt halt in front of him and smiled sweetly.

"I'm *so* sorry I'm late," she said, a little breathless from hurrying. She held a hand out to him. "The traffic on the Drive was unbelievable."

The man looked up from his watch and hesitated, and Melissa let her glance sweep quickly over him. He was not at all what she had expected from his voice on the

1

phone. She had pictured him smallish and a little plump. This man was tall, very tall indeed, with long legs and broad shoulders that seemed to strain the limits of his jacket. He looked like an athlete—a runner. He even, she noticed absently, was wearing white running shoes.

Finally he took her hand and shook it. Melissa felt an abrupt shiver run through her body, as if the touch of his palm against her own had set off some sort of chemical reaction. She blinked once, then politely pulled her hand away.

"It really shouldn't take long," she nattered on, confused by the sensations his touch had set off in her. "We'd like to use the museum for Ransom's alumni dinner, but I do have to look at the facility, and of course we need to talk price." The shivery feeling receded somewhat as she settled back into professionalism.

"Ransom College?"

It was the first time the man had spoken. His voice was deep, deeper than she remembered it on the phone, and Melissa narrowed her eyes quizzically.

He really *wasn't* what she had expected. His face was narrow, with clearly defined cheekbones and deep-set eyes, and his thick dark hair fell into an easy part just off center. He held his head back a little, making his eyes seem almost hooded, even mysterious in the light-and-shadow pattern of the gallery. He was remarkably beautiful, she admitted, surprised.

But also remarkably stupid, she noted impatiently. A public relations man for a huge museum who apparently couldn't remember his own appointments!

"Of course, Ransom College," she said sharply, clicking open the latch on her briefcase with one hand. "I'm Melissa Markham, Ransom's director of development. We spoke on the phone. We had an eleven-thirty appointment? To talk about using the Café for a kickoff dinner for Ransom's fund-raising campaign?"

The man was looking at her, and there was something amused about the tilt of his lips—lips surprisingly full and sensual in a face made up of sharp planes and angles.

"Did we?" he asked.

The truth dawned on her. Melissa pushed the papers she had started to extract from her briefcase back inside. Terrific, she told herself. Now I'm even later. Waylaid by a gorgeous face.

"I've made a mistake," she said flatly. "You're not Tom Burke."

"No." He shook his head, and soft wings of dark hair fell forward on either side of his face. He ran both hands through them, fingers spread, pushing the hair back behind his ears, and he smiled.

Melissa took in a small, sharp breath. He was undeniably gorgeous. Yet the gesture he had just made was entirely without vanity; it was a simple, practical way of getting the offending hair out of his way. It was remarkably appealing and just a little vulnerable, and it seemed to bring an innocence to his hooded eyes.

Melissa smiled back at him in spite of herself.

"No," he repeated, "I'm not. I'm meeting someone here for lunch."

His smile broadened, and he let his gaze meander over Melissa: her thick, shoulder-length auburn curls; her wide-set hazel eyes above a slightly freckled nose and curved mouth; the lines of her breasts, disguised today by her amply cut jacket; and the length of her legs beneath the slim skirt. Then his eyes returned to her face and settled there; she could almost feel his glance brushing her cheek gently, like the wings of a butterfly.

"But I've certainly enjoyed talking with you, Melissa Markham, director of development," he added. "We must do this again sometime."

Melissa forcibly squelched her confusion. "You might have said something a little sooner," she muttered.

"You hardly gave me the chance," he answered with an amused shrug. "But it does appear that the real Mr. Burke is getting a bit restless." He motioned toward the glass doors of the restaurant.

Inside the room, a small, plump man was pacing quickly from table to table, shaking his head and glancing at his watch every step or two. He looked, Melissa thought, exactly like Alice's White Rabbit, with his expression of nervous impatience—and the pocket watch. He was *exactly* what she had expected from his voice on the phone.

Melissa allowed herself one last, sharp glare at the man in the tweed jacket. She knew it wasn't fair to blame him; he was right that she had plunged in headfirst. But still . . . She straightened her shoulders and pushed open the doors.

"Mr. Burke, please forgive me! The traffic on the Drive was absolutely brutal." The plump little man looked at her with an anxious smile.

Forty-five minutes later, arrangements for the dinner in November more or less complete, Melissa left Tom Burke's office and made her way back out through the Terrace Café. She glanced nonchalantly from table to table as she went, but the tall dark man with the electric touch was not to be found.

Chicago's breezes were no longer warm when the night of Ransom's fund-raising dinner actually arrived some eight weeks later. Indian summer had come and gone, and the November wind off the lake was cold, with a hint of snow. Melissa smiled broadly as she scurried up the wide front steps of the museum. The building's massive white facade, sharply outlined against the blackness of the lake, seemed to glow in the night.

Inside the huge marble central hall, a sign directed Ransom guests down to the Terrace Café. Melissa deposited her coat at the checkroom, smoothed her bright-blue jersey dress over her hips, and headed for the Café. The first arrivals were already standing in small clusters amid the sculpture outside the restaurant.

Melissa said a quick hello to Katherine McAllister, the silver-haired woman checking people in, then made her way through the room. She pumped hands and checked name tags, all the while flipping through mental note cards so she would say just the right thing to just the right person, making everyone comfortable. Doing her job.

Then she led the way into the Café itself. It was as perfect as the White Rabbit had promised: Round tables were set with crisp white linen and bowls of red and white flowers; shiny ceramic apples and strings of tiny white lights hung from the potted trees that dotted the room; a well-supplied bar and cocktail buffet were set up unobtrusively against one wall; and overhead, the high glass roof showed a dazzle of stars flung like sequins against the clear night sky. Perfect.

When the alumni began to mingle on their own, Melissa ducked out again to the gallery, where Katherine McAllister sat at a small desk next to a life-sized sculpted bed with two disconsolate-looking people on it. Melissa watched for a moment as the woman crossed off names from her invitation list with one hand and sought out an errant name tag with the other.

"Katherine," she said when there was a break in the action, "you're looking very efficient! How're we doing?"

"Hello again, Lissie!" Katherine, whose elegant gray suit almost exactly matched her hair, looked up and smiled. "We're doing very nicely indeed. Almost half already here—even some of the question marks."

Melissa glanced down the invitation list and nodded. Hard work was paying off: It was a good turnout.

"Now if only we can sweet-talk these folks into handing over their wallets!" she said lightly.

Katherine smiled. "Alan's in there doing his best," she said, gesturing toward the Café.

Melissa laughed. "Kath, what I wouldn't give for a hundred Alan and Katherine McAllisters." She patted her friend's shoulder and turned away.

For the next thirty minutes, Melissa made the rounds. The basic campaign had been mapped out before she'd been hired at Ransom, six months earlier, but in every other way it was her baby. The college had met nearly half its goal already through big lump-sum donations from major alumni and corporations, and Alan McAllister had taken his position as volunteer chairman very seriously. But tonight was the public kickoff—the first time many of the alumni would really have a chance to hear about the campaign in detail—and it was vitally important. Melissa moved from group to group, talking about Ransom's needs, gearing her pitch to what she knew about the people around her.

With fifteen minutes left before dinner, Melissa headed back to Katherine's desk and stood in front of it, peering at the upside-down invitation list.

She nodded, pleased. "It really looks good," she began, but Katherine gave her arm a sudden sharp poke.

"Who is *that?*" Katherine interrupted in a frankly curious whisper.

Melissa, still leaning over the desk, glanced over her shoulder.

The elevator doors on the opposite side of the gallery had opened, and a tall man with dark hair and broad shoulders was emerging, as if exploding from a cage that was too small for him.

The same man she'd met there two months earlier. He hesitated for a moment at the elevator doors, and the hint of a smile on his mouth left no doubt in Melissa's mind that he was enjoying the sight of her leaning over the desk, her blue jersey dress molded to her hips. She straightened up quickly.

Theirs had been a chance encounter, and she had pushed it as far as possible into the recesses of her mind. But she had found, much to her annoyance, that she couldn't entirely get rid of the memory. In fact, during the past eight weeks, the tall dark man now coming toward them had played roles in her dreams that she wouldn't want to repeat in public. She rubbed suddenly damp palms against her dress.

"He must work for the Art Institute," she said in an uncertain voice. "I've seen him here before."

"Pity," Katherine said brightly. "I kind of hoped he was one of ours." She sent a welcoming smile in his direction.

The man approached them through the patterns of light and shadow designed to show off the sculpture. There was something almost dreamlike, Melissa thought, about watching him move among the immobile art. He was wearing a perfectly cut gray jacket, a proper white shirt, and a Ransom red tie. But his long legs were encased in faded blue jeans, and on his feet were white running shoes with a stylized slash of golden lightning down the side of each one. Very fashionable, she told herself dryly.

"Hello again," he said. He stopped next to the realistic bed with its two uncommunicative occupants. His dark glance caught Melissa's and held it firmly.

Melissa ducked her head in a confused nod that she hoped passed for polite greeting.

"Can we help?" Katherine was looking up at the man with open admiration. Her voice broke the awkward silence like the cavalry coming to the rescue.

"I hope so," the man said pleasantly. He shifted his gaze to Katherine and leaned forward to read her name tag. "Mrs. McAllister," he added. "My name's Dakin Quarry. I should be on your list." He pulled a cream-colored invitation from his jacket pocket.

"Quarry," Katherine repeated. "Dakin. What an unusual name." She ran a pencil down her list.

The name clicked in Melissa's head. No reservation, but there was a star next to his name on the list—he was one of those targeted by the staff for special attention. The star meant they'd sent a second and maybe even a third invitation.

Terrific, Markham, she told herself. You've already acted like an idiot in front of one of the evening's biggest catches.

"Mr. Quarry," she said with a forced smile, "I'm

afraid the last time we met..." She cleared her throat and started again. "I had no idea you had any connection with Ransom."

The small smile was still on his face. "I don't suppose I look like the typical Ransom product," he said with a deprecating wave at his jeans.

Melissa tossed her head a little stiffly. "There's no such thing," she heard herself say as she belatedly gathered her professional cloak around herself. "Ransom's student body is extremely diverse. In any case, we're delighted you could make it. I don't think we had a reservation..."

"No. I just decided to come. Am I allowed in?"

"Well, of course," Katherine said happily. "And welcome."

"You just decided?" Melissa repeated. Something deep inside her seemed to be rousing itself from a long sleep, and she shifted her weight from one foot to the other.

Dakin Quarry nodded. "Just this afternoon," he said. "But I've been thinking about it for a while."

Then, for the first time, his little smile broadened, and the mysteries of his dark face seemed suddenly resolved. Melissa blinked. It was a remarkable smile—bright white teeth against the bronze planes of his face—and it brought an animation to his sensual features that was almost mischievous.

The full force of his generous smile surged at Melissa, and she had the distinct sense he was quite sure he had made the right decision in coming.

She leaned over the desk so her thick hair fell forward, covering the pink tint she knew had invaded her cheeks, and ran a pencil down the invitation list. Quarry, she repeated to herself, Quarry. Frantically, she asked her usually efficient mind to come up with something—some piece of information about the man standing in front of her—but she drew a complete blank. She had no idea why her staff had marked him with a star.

Katherine McAllister filled the conversational void.

"I don't think I've heard your name before," she said. "I'm sure I'd have remembered it. Are you from Chicago, Mr. Quarry?"

He shook his head. "I've only been in the area about three years. I own a plant a bit west of here. Near Elgin." He looked from Katherine to Melissa and back again. "And please call me Dake," he added.

"Dake," Katherine repeated with a grin.

Near Elgin. What *was* it he did? Melissa frowned. At least, she told herself, *talk* to the man. Do your job. But her brain simply refused to engage itself.

"Well, we're certainly glad to welcome you, Dake," Katherine said with a smile, handing him a name tag, "but I'm afraid we'll have to ask you to pay for your supper."

Dake pinned the name tag carefully to the lapel of his jacket. "Of course," he said. "How much do I owe the cause?"

"Twenty dollars." Katherine opened a small metal box that sat on one side of the desk. "Unless you'd like to add a little something for the campaign," she went on. "Melissa's decided we need to raise nine million dollars in the next two years." Her gaze skimmed Quarry's long, lithe body, and she snapped her fingers. "You must have been an athlete," she went on. "You might want to earmark your contribution for the new stadium."

Dake had one hand in his inside jacket pocket, reaching for his wallet, and he stopped with it there.

"Something wrong with the old one?" he asked.

"Actually it *is* the old one," Melissa corrected quickly, relieved to be once again capable of joining the conversation. "We're just planning some renovations. It's a fairly small part of the campaign. Ransom hasn't had a major gifts campaign in recent memory, and we'd like to get the endowment back up to full strength."

She tried to repress her annoyance at setting money aside for the stadium, but she did disapprove of the importance of athletics in college fund-raising. Realistically, however, she knew it was often sports that made people give money. If she had her way, every penny of this campaign would go for student assistance, faculty compensation, and library funds.

Dake was looking at her steadily, and the tension of his pose cut abruptly into her thoughts. His hand was still frozen half inside his jacket. He looked as if he were a permanent part of the gallery.

"When it's done," Katherine chirped on, oblivious to the changed atmosphere, "it's probably going to be renamed after Bob Rudge. You must remember Coach Rudge if you were a Ransom athlete."

Dake's hand remained where it was. His face had become sharp, hard-edged, the way soft, fresh snow on a ski run suddenly turns out to be, on closer view, glittering, unwelcome ice. And you're already going too fast, Melissa thought, to avoid it.

"Robert Rudge Stadium," he said slowly. "I see."

"It's really a very small percentage—" Melissa began.

"I think I'll pass on the stadium fund," he said. He pulled his wallet from his pocket, his fluid motions thawing as quickly as they had frozen, and laid two ten-dollar bills on the desk.

Melissa started to respond, to say once again that the campaign was much, much more than a stadium fund, but something stopped her. She was curious about Dakin Quarry. His incredible physical appeal was not the only source of her interest; she was professionally curious as well. But the mental note cards continued to come up blank, and she wanted to know everything about him before she made her pitch.

She allowed herself a small grin. Well, maybe not *everything*.

"We're all set then," Katherine said, tucking the cash into the metal box. "Why don't you two go on in? I'll finish up out here." The older woman smiled warmly at them both.

Abruptly, the shivery feeling was back. It started in

Melissa's stomach this time and spread slowly outward, reaching into every limb, every finger, every toe. She stood rooted to the floor, one hand on the desk to support herself. Dake held out an arm for her to take.

Melissa shook her head sharply. "I . . . I should probably go over the list one more time," she muttered.

"Nonsense," Katherine said firmly. "It's all under control. There can't possibly be more than two or three people who haven't yet arrived."

Dake watched Melissa with a broad smile, clearly amused at her reticence.

"Come on, Mel," he said. "You must have work to do in there."

Melissa blinked. No one had ever called her Mel before, and she kind of liked the sound of it. It made her sound grown-up, somehow—not like little-girl Lissie. Still, she tucked her hands deep into the pockets of her wraparound dress. She knew if she took Dake Quarry's proffered arm, she would have trouble keeping her footing.

"Why, yes," she said. She let the smile that had more than once been called dazzling settle on her lips. "Yes, I do. Money to raise, goals to meet." She gazed one last time around the gallery, feeling as if the large pieces of sculpture were somehow old friends. "Let's go."

It was hard to ignore the man next to her—his height, the width of his angular shoulders, the obvious strength of his body. She could almost feel the warmth of him as the sleeve of his jacket brushed against her arm. She cleared her throat.

Just remember, she lectured herself, this guy is a big potential target. And it's your business to get the most out of that potential.

"Very nice," Dake said as they made their way through the restaurant toward the bar. "So this is what you arranged when you were here in September?"

Melissa nodded. "The White Rabbit really did a fine job," she said.

Dake glanced down at her. "The White Rabbit?"

A smile played at the corners of her mouth. "Mr. Burke," she said. "The man who was pacing in here that day. He reminded me of the White Rabbit."

Dake nodded thoughtfully. "And you're obviously Alice," he responded. "So who am I?"

Melissa shot him a quick glance. "Why am I Alice?" she asked. It was uncanny, how rattled he could make her feel with the simplest of remarks.

Dake smiled at her. "I don't know," he said. "Your hair, maybe. Or the way you seem thrown by the unexpected."

"Get you something?" the bartender interrupted.

"Ginger ale," Melissa answered quickly. Dake ordered a Scotch for himself.

"So who am I?" he asked again.

He looked down at Melissa, and his dark eyes were wide now, without the vaguely lazy look they had had earlier. They seemed to reflect the soft sheen of the night and the stars that glittered overhead, muted softly by the glass roof.

"Good question," she said weakly. Ask him what he does, she told herself sharply. Ask him when he graduated. Ask him *something*. Tell him he's the Mad Hatter. Don't just stand here and gape.

But she couldn't take her eyes off his. If he asked me to lie down right there and make love with him, she thought abruptly, I believe I'd do it.

"Dake," she said finally, pushing every word out carefully, "I really should make the rounds before they actually serve dinner. If you'll excuse me. Maybe we can talk later." She sent him a bright smile and turned away.

He caught her arm with his hand. "Why don't I just tag along?" he asked casually. "I'd enjoy watching you work."

Melissa blew a tiny breath out and pushed her heavy auburn hair away from her face. Then she nodded and led him to a small circle of men that included Katherine

McAllister's husband, Alan. The men were bemoaning the cost of housing in the area. They paused long enough to greet Melissa and be introduced to Dake.

"You know," Melissa inserted at the first opportunity, "this economic situation hits everyone. We're getting a much higher percentage of students at Ransom who need some form of aid, and—"

"And Ransom actually feels some obligation to provide it?" a deep voice interrupted from beside her. Melissa glanced at Dake. His head was thrown slightly back again, his eyes hooded and lazy.

The other men were studying Dake in the way Melissa had often seen wealthy men size up a newcomer: eyes slightly narrowed in neutral faces, making no commitments until they had assessed his value.

"Of course," she said firmly. "Ransom has always felt an obligation to the needy student. Obviously, not every bright kid can pay his or her way through college."

"Obviously." Dake nodded thoughtfully. "And sometimes, of course, those needy students are useful to the college as well."

The smooth hair fell forward again. He pushed it back, and Melissa wondered suddenly what it would be like to do that herself—to push that thick black hair back from Dakin Quarry's forehead with the palms of her hands. Would it feel smooth against her skin? Would it glide through her fingers softly, like summer grass grown a little too long? She shook her head, trying to get rid of the image, as warmth flooded into her cheeks.

"Forty percent of Ransom students have some kind of loan or direct grant from the college," she said automatically, pulling the familiar words out of storage, "and many more have low-cost federal loans or some other—"

"What percentage of this money you're asking for tonight will actually go to students who need it?" Dake asked. There was a hard edge to his voice. "And what percentage will go toward Mr. Rudge's stadium?"

Alan McAllister looked at Dake, clearly interested. The others were still refusing to commit themselves.

"The stadium will take only about five percent—" Melissa began, but a familiar voice broke in.

"Talking about my stadium?"

Melissa felt a twinge of impatience. Dake clearly wanted an honest answer, and she wasn't at all sure he'd get one from Bob Rudge. Theoretically, Rudge was a great plus for Ransom and for Melissa: A popular football and track coach, he was also the college's athletic director, with a long string of winning seasons to his credit. So why, she wondered, did he annoy her so much? In the six months she'd been doing the job, there was no one she had come to like less.

She turned to him with a forced smile.

"Hello, Bob. Actually we were talking about *all* of Ransom's needs." She knew her refusal to call him Coach, as he urged everyone to do, irritated him, and she took a certain perverse pleasure in that.

Rudge inserted his portly body into the circle. He gave the odd appearance of rolling as he moved, as if he were a collection of rubber beach balls. He was one of those unfortunate ex–football players whose muscle had turned to ooze.

"Terrific!" he said, his voice a little breathy from the effort of moving across the room. "Happy to see you all. Alan." He reached across the circle and shook hands with Alan McAllister, then strained to read the name tags on the other men and nodded to them in turn.

"Well," he wheezed as he reached Dake, "Dakin Quarry. Now *that's* a name I've been seeing a lot of lately, sir. Never forget a name. I see by the papers you've been doing pretty well for yourself."

Melissa looked at Dake. He was standing immobile, and his height seemed to dominate the little circle. He looked coldly at the man across from him. He resembled, Melissa thought, the man on the bed in the sculpture gallery—frozen in an attitude of hard disappointment.

Melissa sensed an impending crisis, and she knew it was her job to avert it.

"Do you know Mr. Quarry, Bob?" she asked. Terrific question, she told herself sharply. He just *said* he knows him.

"Man invented Windflame track shoes, darlin'," Rudge announced. He winked at Dake, apparently oblivious to Dake's iciness. "Big sellers. You're probably about to come up on a lot of profits, say what, Dake?"

The other men looked curious now, too. They were, Melissa knew, ready to dismiss their disapproval of his jeans and sneakers if they could be shown that Dake Quarry had the right kind of business sense and the right amount of money in the bank. Only Alan McAllister looked sincerely interested, and the little frown between his sandy eyebrows signaled that he shared Melissa's concern over the situation that seemed to be brewing.

"Coach Rudge," Alan asked before the other men had noticed the silence, "tell these folks what's going to happen with the Northwestern game this year."

Rudge glanced from Quarry to McAllister, then shrugged and smiled slowly. "Gonna get 'em this year, Alan. Gonna cream 'em."

Melissa shot a grateful glance at Alan as the conversation sprang to life again. Only Dake had nothing to say about the two games left in the Ransom football schedule.

She lowered her eyes to the floor and took a deep breath. She would have to remember to thank Alan later; it was a job she should have done herself. But Dake Quarry, she had to admit, seemed to throw her off-balance. In every way.

The men chattered on, and Melissa let her gaze move around the circle, from one set of dark brown shoes to the next, until the white of Dake's sneakers with the golden lightning bolts down the sides caught her attention. A smile turned up the corners of her lips. That was the missing piece of information, of course. He made running shoes that were fast becoming the most popular brand in the country. No wonder he was wearing sneakers to a formal dinner.

Slowly her gaze traveled up the long legs, the lithe, muscular thighs encased in jeans the color of a pale spring sky, over the slender hips and waist. His jacket had one button fastened; creamy white shirt front, split by his red tie, showed above it. Absently, she wondered if his broad chest was smooth or if there was a drift of dark down across it.

Her eyes reached his face. He was watching her watch him, and he was smiling. Melissa felt her knees weaken, and she took a little shuffling step to the left. Her arm bumped Bob Rudge's.

"Now you, Dake," Rudge's voice boomed, his attention back on the younger man, "you ran track for us, what about fifteen years ago, wasn't it, sir?"

Melissa turned abruptly toward the coach. She was aware that Dake was nodding, and she felt irrationally grateful that he was finally making *some* response, even just a nod.

"Damn good, the boy was." Rudge looked around the circle, confirming his pronouncement by locking eyes with everyone there. "Even some talk about the Olympics, wasn't there, sir? Or a Rhodes? Maybe not." He shook his head, and his chins followed one after the other like baby ducks tripping after their mother. "So what's been up since then, sir? What've you been doing, besides coining money?" Rudge laughed, a brief, explosive burst that was over almost as soon as it had begun.

Dake Quarry stood still for one more moment. The rest of the men looked at him curiously, and he let his gaze roam once around the circle.

"I've been recovering," he finally said in a voice that was steady and deep, "from Ransom College."

Then he turned and strode deliberately toward the exit.

There was a silence in the group that lasted until his wide-shouldered silhouette had become a shadow among the other shadows in the sculpture gallery. Melissa's eyes followed his path; she watched him move past the life-size bed, then out of sight.

"That guy," Bob Rudge finally said with another shake of his head, "was the biggest spoiled brat I ever tried to coach. Thought he was the greatest thing since sliced bread. Finally had to take his scholarship away from him, but I guess he never did learn to be civil."

Melissa continued to study the view through the glass doors. Dakin Quarry didn't reappear, but his image seemed to hang in the shadows: the angular width of his shoulders, the straight-cut black hair swinging ever so slightly below the collar of his gray jacket, the pale-blue jeans hugging his long legs. She could even see the small golden lightning bolts on his shoes.

The image slowly faded, until only his smile remained. The Cheshire Cat, Melissa thought suddenly. If I'm Alice, then you're the Cheshire Cat.

- 2 -

"BEST PRESENTATION I'VE heard from you yet," President Warren announced, giving Melissa's hand a firm shake. The few remaining guests were gathering their coats from a tired-looking checkroom clerk in the marble lobby of the museum.

Melissa nodded and smiled. She felt exhausted, as much, she had to admit, from the effort of not thinking about Dakin Quarry after his precipitous departure as by the dinner itself. Objectively, she knew, the evening had gone very well.

Alan McAllister returned from the checkroom with an armful of coats. "Great idea," he said, handing Melissa hers, "having this shindig here. I have to admit it's the first time I've been here in fifteen years."

His wife looked at him darkly. "Alan," she said, "how embarrassing!" Then she brightened. "Well, *I* have. The girls used to take classes here on Saturdays."

Alan grinned at Melissa. "I hope you made millions," he said.

Melissa smiled warmly. "You've gotten us off to a

19

good start, Alan—you and your cronies. I'll try to keep it going."

"And I'll do what I can. But for now, let us walk you to your car." Alan put a hand on his wife's arm and another on Melissa's, and started for the door. "You've got our parking ticket, don't you, Kath?"

Katherine clicked open her purse, and Melissa heard her take a quick breath of surprise.

"Lissie," she said, leaning across her husband, "I absolutely forgot. I have something for you."

She pulled a folded piece of paper from her purse and handed it to Melissa.

"That man—the one with the marvelous shoulders. Dakin Quarry. He gave me this for you. What happened to him, anyway?"

Melissa stared at her. "When?" she asked softly. "When did he give you this?"

They were standing at the top of the broad front steps of the museum, and the wind off the lake was chilling. Katherine tilted her head to one side.

"He came stalking out of the restaurant and right by me—not a good-bye or anything. He must have been all the way outside, and then he just appeared again. He handed me this note and said to give it to you." She smiled mischievously. "What's it say, Lissie?"

Melissa's gloves made her fingers awkward. Alan had already started down the steps; now he stopped and turned.

"What's going on?" he called.

"Just a minute," Katherine called back. "What *is* it?" she asked again.

Melissa pulled it open. The message was simple: *Palmer House. Room 1222.* She blinked once, then crumpled it into her own purse.

"His hotel room," she said dryly. "Tacky."

Katherine had the grace to look just a little shocked. "Well . . ." she began uncertainly.

"Tacky," Melissa repeated firmly. "And I'm exhausted. Thanks again, Kath, for all your help." She scurried on down the steps, tossing a good-bye to Alan as she skipped by him, then headed across Michigan Avenue before he could insist on seeing her to her car.

She felt something close to elation, a lightness she had never felt before, as though if she weren't careful about where she stepped, she might float right on up among the skyscrapers. She glanced north toward the lofty John Hancock Building and grinned.

Melissa covered the single block of Adams Street in quick, long strides, then turned right up Wabash. I have a reason to be going this way, she told herself firmly; my car is halfway up this block. But straight ahead, on the corner of Wabash and Monroe, sat the Palmer House Hotel, matronly and massive, its brightly lit facade welcoming in the dark night.

Her steps slowed as she reached the lot that held her car, but almost without instruction her feet kept on moving.

"Damn," she muttered. "This is not smart."

She glanced at her watch. Eleven-thirty. Not *too* late. She hesitated for a moment and glanced back at the parking lot, now well behind her. Then, with a deep breath, she loped across Wabash just ahead of the light, ignoring the honking taxi that had started across the intersection early, and took refuge in the ground floor arcade of Chicago's Grand Old Lady.

The smart thing, she told herself, would be to turn back, go to her car, and drive away. Go home. Leave Dake Quarry alone—at least, as she had promised herself earlier in the evening, until she knew a little more about him.

But she felt a certain professional challenge, an itch to learn the story from Dake himself. She stepped onto the escalator up to the main lobby. Maybe, after all, he wanted to talk about making a contribution. Maybe he'd changed his mind about the campaign.

Right. Melissa laughed as she pushed the button for the elevator. First she'd come barreling up to him out of nowhere and made a fool of herself, and then she'd stood blithely by as he made mincemeat out of her dinner. He just had to be impressed with her efficiency as a fund-raiser.

She stepped into the elevator and pushed twelve. Two laughing couples hurried on just as the doors were closing. They got off at five. Melissa stayed on.

Damn, she told herself again. You are not usually this dumb.

The doors opened at twelve, and Melissa looked out into the empty hallway, a little eerie at this time of night. There's still time, she thought. All I have to do is wait until the doors close, and then push LOBBY.

She stepped off and checked the direction sign, then turned to the right. Her footsteps slowed a little as she passed 1218, then 1220. At 1222 she hesitated, opened her purse, and checked the room number against the one on the note.

Face it, she told herself, this man does *not* want to contribute to your campaign. He has made that abundantly clear. And, to be fair, that's not precisely what you want from him, either. Go home. Right now.

She raised a hand and knocked once.

For a moment there was no sound. A smile tugged at the corners of her mouth. Ransom's bad boy, already asleep at eleven-thirty at night. She started to turn away.

Then the door swung quietly open, and Dake Quarry stood smiling at her from the other side.

Melissa cleared her throat, disguising the little gulp she couldn't altogether stop. He had shed his jacket and tie and rolled the sleeves of his white shirt midway up his forearms. His arms were smooth and tan, and his waist and hips seemed even leaner without his jacket. But the faded denim of his jeans pulled tight across thighs more muscular than she had realized.

Her eyes traveled unbidden down the length of his body and came to rest at his bare feet. There was something remarkably affecting about them, the grace of the

high arches and long lines—and a sudden sense of nakedness.

She glanced across the rug. A single lamp by the bed
cast a soft glow around the room, and his white running
shoes sat on the floor just beneath it. The golden lightning
bolts seemed to shimmer in the semi-darkness.

Dake was still smiling.

"Melissa Markham, director of development," he said,
drawing out the syllables with a faintly Western lilt. "How
nice to see you again."

He had one hand on the doorknob, and he bowed from
the waist. Melissa stepped quickly into the room before
she could change her mind and flee.

"I was afraid you wouldn't come," he said softly as
she moved by him.

"I just got your message." Her voice was as nervously
brisk as her footsteps. "Such as it was."

"Sorry if the invitation wasn't to your liking," he said,
pushing the door shut and leaning back against it. "No
time to get it engraved, I'm afraid."

Melissa had stopped a few feet from him, and he
straightened up, stepped behind her, and slid her coat off
her shoulders. His hands barely brushed the fabric of her
dress, but Melissa could feel the familiar shiver begin
again somewhere deep inside. This time there was a
power in it she hadn't felt before. Dake tossed her coat
onto a chair by the door, and she turned to look at him.

"You did seem rather in a hurry to get away," she said
dryly.

"Robert Rudge has always had that effect on me."

He leaned against the door again and jammed one
hand into the back pocket of his jeans. He glanced at his
watch. It was precisely the pose she had first seen him
in, way back when. The shivery feeling moved slowly
upward, and she felt a sudden heaviness in her breasts.
She took a deep breath.

You are acting like an eighteen-year-old, she told herself sternly. Absolutely like a teenager.

"Well," she said, making a conscious effort to smile, "I assume you want to talk about giving Ransom some money. Yes?"

He looked at her for a moment, eyebrows raised, and then threw his head back and laughed. It was the first time she had heard him laugh, and the warm, comfortable sound startled her. Instinctively, she laughed, too. It was remarkable, she thought as she had earlier in the evening, how his broad smile changed his face—from dangerous mountain cat to friendly puppy.

"No," he said finally, "I'm not quite there yet. Will you run away if I tell you I'm more interested in you than in your job?"

Melissa shrugged. "I won't run away. But," she added with a smile, "it might make a difference in the degree of my interest in *you*."

Dake tipped his head a little, and the hooded, mysterious look returned. "Ah. Well, I did want to apologize. For running out on your party. I hope it didn't make the evening too difficult for you."

She shrugged again, although the liquid heaviness inside had now replaced the wonderful airy lightness she had felt out on the street, and it was hard to seem casual and carefree.

"I really don't think many people noticed," she said.

She glanced around the room. The queen-size bed with its peach-colored satiny spread seemed to take up all the available space, and Melissa tried to find other things to look at.

"How disappointing." Dake moved away from the door and into her line of vision again. His gaze rested steadily on her face, and his look was challenging, almost arrogant. "Not even Bob Rudge?"

"Oh . . . well, yes." She nodded and smiled. "Yes, Bob noticed."

"Said something, did he?"

Melissa looked at him. "Dake," she said, "if you have some old fight to pick—"

"Sit down," he quietly interrupted.

Melissa blinked. He had moved a step or two closer, and now he stood between her and the door. He was smiling his wide, comfortable smile, and Melissa found herself smiling back. He gestured toward a small couch in front of the curtained windows at the far end of the room.

"I—"

"Sit down," he repeated.

She walked to the couch and sat, feeling a flurry of nervousness. Outside the room everything seemed still; only faint traffic noises carried up from the street twelve stories below. It was as if she and Dake existed in some elegant cocoon—just the two of them. An exhilarating sense of anticipation joined the nervousness, but Melissa wasn't at all sure what she was anticipating.

"Is my apology accepted?" he asked.

She looked up at him. His large eyes were almost lost in the darkness above his high cheekbones, and everything about him seemed sharp and mysterious, even frightening. But she wasn't frightened. She was excited. She ran her tongue over her dry lips.

Then he lowered his head a little to look at her, and his dark hair fell forward. He lifted both hands and pushed it back. Like a farmer, she thought suddenly—the way a farmer might push his hair back in the middle of a hot field. She laughed softly.

"Apology accepted," she said.

He looked at her for a moment longer, eyebrows slightly raised in curiosity, then turned away. "How about some wine?" he asked. "This room comes stocked with some remarkably bad California."

Melissa settled back against the couch with a feeling of relief. You're doing fine, she told herself happily. He's just a regular man—even if he does make your stomach do flipflops.

"That would be great. *Anything* would be great. I don't drink when I'm on duty."

Dake glanced over his shoulder at her as he poured two glasses of wine. "You mean you can keep that incredible smile on your face for five hours at a stretch without the aid of alcohol or drugs?"

She laughed. "Sometimes it's tough," she admitted. "The toughest is when some guy thinks that because you're asking him for money, he's entitled to—" She stopped, suddenly uncomfortable.

"Entitled to something in return?" Dake finished for her. He handed her a glass of wine.

She sipped gratefully and nodded.

"They have trouble keeping the profession separate from the person?"

Melissa nodded again. "Something like that. It can be a thin line."

Dake seemed to watch her thoughtfully as he sipped from his own glass. He let his eyes rake casually over her—the soft curve of her breasts where her wrap dress came together in a V, the line of her crossed knees where the dress had fallen open. Melissa pulled it primly closed again.

"I can see where that would be a problem," he said, his voice amused. "How about you?"

She looked up at him. "How about me what?"

"How do *you* keep the two separate? What if you find a man who attracts you among the . . . what do you call us? Clients?"

"Targets," she answered automatically. "I . . . I haven't had that come up. Yet."

Dake held the thin stem of his glass between his palms and rolled it back and forth; it caught the light from the single lamp and threw glimmers of crystal off into the air. Melissa suddenly wanted to swat at the shimmering streaks of light, to rip through the tangible tension in the air with her hand, to shatter whatever it was that was making the back of her neck tingle.

Then Dake laughed. The sound was as refreshing and reassuring as it had been the first time. He pulled a chair away from the wall and sat in it, facing her.

"Well, Mel Markham, director of development, I'm glad you decided to come and relax with me. I've wanted to know more about you since you first came panting up to me and introduced yourself, lo these many long weeks ago. So tell me how you got started in this line of work."

"You mean development?"

"I mean asking people for their money. Whatever it's called."

Melissa smiled. "Sometimes I think I was born doing it. I used to go around my neighborhood when I was a kid, asking for donations for the starving kids in . . . wherever it was at the moment. Then when I graduated from Ransom, I married a doctor, so volunteering for charity work was part of the deal. Very socially acceptable." She made a face, and Dake smiled.

"But you kept at it," he said.

"Mmm. I found I still liked it. As long as I really cared about the cause. And I was good at it."

This is not, Melissa told herself, what is supposed to be happening. I came up here to find out about *him*.

"And how did *you* get started making shoes?" she asked.

"You really care about Ransom College?" He looked at her steadily, his eyes pools of darkness in the dim light, as he ignored her question altogether.

Melissa took a sip of her wine. "Yes," she said after a moment. "Yes, I do. I got what I consider a very good education there. And you, I gather, didn't."

"Oh, the education was just fine," he responded quickly. The small smile was on his lips again. "What I got of it."

Suddenly he leaned forward in his chair, resting his elbows on his knees, and dangled his glass dangerously from one hand. "What happened to your doctor, Mel?" he asked bluntly.

Melissa could feel his abrupt closeness, his knees just a foot or so from hers, the features of his face now clear and intense. She pulled air deep into her lungs and let it out slowly. Dake settled back again, his glass still dangling from the fingers of one hand, and she relaxed a bit.

It's getting late, she told herself firmly. You should just get up and leave.

"My husband didn't like it when the volunteer work turned into a career," she said steadily.

Dake raised an eyebrow. "That's it?"

"Of course not. But that's the easiest explanation. And it's true. He had trouble seeing the distinction between person and profession, too. All he knew was that his wife was out there making money by asking people—generally men—for it. It seemed a little . . ." She brought her eyebrows together in a frown. "Disreputable."

Dake shook his head. "But you're doing good—theoretically—for other people. Just the way a doctor does."

Melissa shrugged. "He didn't see it that way." She shifted her weight. The tingling in her nape was almost gone. "What about you?" she asked again, more aggressively this time. "Where did you appear from? Even Katherine McAllister's never heard of you, and she knows every breathing, money-making soul in Chicago."

Dake grinned. "Ah, here it comes."

"What's *that* supposed to mean?"

"The pitch. What is it that you do exactly, Dake? How much money do you make from it? How much can we wheedle away from you for the cause?"

Melissa sat silently for a moment. "That's twaddle," she said finally. Then she smiled. "In any case, for you I'd use a much subtler approach. You've already let me know you have some problems with Ransom College."

He looked at her and grinned. "Okay. I'll give you a fair start. I came from Colorado. A little town in the northeast corner called Brush. My parents raised sugar beets. Ransom gave me an athletic scholarship because I held the national junior title in the four-forty when I was in high school, and I took it instead of Colorado

State because I wanted to see what a city looked like. After college I did a little of this and a little of that, played some basketball in Europe, and a couple of years ago I started selling a running shoe I'd designed. My factory's out near Elgin. Enough?"

Melissa looked at him curiously. He *was* a farmer, to begin with. It was funny, the sensation she had had earlier about that little gesture of his.

"Not enough," he said when she remained silent. "Okay. Let's see. I was married once, briefly, a long time ago. No children. Windflame Runners are very popular all of a sudden. My factory grosses . . . Do you want the figures?"

Melissa shook her head. She knew she was grinning. "That's enough to start," she said. So he was single. And he was gorgeous. And she was feeling something deeper and richer, way down inside, than she had ever before felt about a man she had just met. Something so deep it was almost painful. The grin on her face, she thought, must look absolutely daffy.

Time to go, she told herself abruptly.

She started to rise, and Dake rose, too.

"If you just wanted to apologize . . ." she began uncertainly.

"That's not all I wanted, Mel," he countered.

Melissa let herself fall back against the couch, all too conscious of how close their bodies would be if they were both on their feet. She looked up at him. His shoulders seemed to fill the space above her completely, leaving no room for light or shadow or even air. Almost at her eye level his white shirt had pulled open just a little, and she could see a tiny triangle of smooth golden skin above the belt of his jeans. She felt a sudden wave of giddiness, and she grabbed hold of the arm of the couch.

"Why did you come here, Mel?" he asked softly, his voice almost a whisper.

"I . . ." She held the arm of the couch tightly and straightened her shoulders. "Why did *you* come to the dinner?" she responded, challenging. "When you dislike Ransom so much?"

He looked down at her. "There's a hard answer and an easy one. The hard answer is, because I thought it was time to give Ransom another chance. The easy one is, because I wanted to see you again."

He reached over and set his wineglass down on a nearby table, then took hers from her hand and deposited it there, too. Then he rested both his hands on her shoulders, and suddenly they were joined together, a single fluid being.

The touch was expected, but Melissa jumped as if a spark had leaped from an open fire. She could feel the heat of his strong hands through the thin jersey of her dress. She started to rise, to shake off his hands, but Dake used her own action to pull her to her feet. Suddenly, without meaning to be there, Melissa was standing in front of him, their bodies so close that she could feel his warmth up and down the length of her.

"Dake, this is—"

The pressure of his mouth silenced her. His lips were hot against her own, and she was aware of their fullness as they moved softly over her face, touching her cheeks, her eyelids, her chin, always returning to her mouth and finally settling there. It was exactly as she had dreamed during those weeks after she had first seen him; those sensual lips were hard but yielding, urgent against her own. The shivery feeling took over her whole body, and suddenly her legs felt rubbery.

Dake's hand circled her throat, his thumb against her cheek. She rubbed her face against his hand as a cat might. That single hand supported her. His mouth moved against hers, and Melissa knew that her own lips were moving in response, opening for him, letting him have his way. There was nothing, she thought desperately, she could do to stop him.

And she didn't want to. His tongue sought hers, and she shuddered again, liking the tickle of it at her teeth, the exquisite pleasure of it playing against the inside of her cheeks. Her own tongue responded, seeking the sweet recesses of his mouth. He tasted of wine.

The pressure of his body was hard against her own, his broad chest against her full, firm breasts. Melissa could feel the cordlike muscles of his thighs as he moved one leg slightly and the fabric of her wrapped skirt fell open. The worn denim of his jeans made a little hissing sound as it rubbed against her stocking.

He slid one hand inside the V of her dress, brushing the back of it across the top of her breasts. The heavy, liquid heat she had felt earlier flooded through her again, stronger now, and the fullness in her breasts made her lean more heavily against the tall, strong body before her. His hand moved slowly down, into the hollow between her breasts.

Melissa pulled in a deep breath. It felt like the air along the lake shore when she ran in the early morning—clean and cool and just a little tart. She was suddenly filled with the luxurious ease she always felt when she had run a long distance, the feeling of comfort within her body, of comfort with her body.

Now the pressure against her was almost unbearable—against her mouth, her breasts, her thighs, all along the length of her body. She felt Dake take a step backward, then another, keeping her always within the strong circle of his arms. Behind him she could see, when she opened her eyes, the gleaming satin coverlet of the bed. Her eyes opened wide.

What the hell are you doing, Markham? she asked herself abruptly. In a hotel room, with some man you don't really know . . .

She took a quick step back and grasped his wrists, pulling his hands away from her. She shook her head fiercely.

Dake looked at her, his eyes wide and dark in the soft light. He looked golden and perfect, and his hair had fallen forward. He didn't bother to push it back. Melissa felt the beginning of an ache somewhere at the very center of her being.

After a moment, he pulled his hands free from her grasp. Softly, gently, he lifted her hands to his mouth, first one and then the other, and kissed their palms. The touch of his lips was like the touch of a warm summer breeze, but it was a breeze that threatened to become a hurricane, a whirlwind on the great western plains. Melissa looked down.

"Problems?" Dake whispered.

She dropped her hands to her sides and fought to keep her balance on undependable legs. Finally she nodded.

"I find you very attractive," she said softly. Her eyes remained on the floor, but she sensed that he was smiling.

"Clearly, the feeling is mutual," he said. "Go on."

Melissa took another deep breath. This time the air was easily identifiable: the air of a hotel room in the middle of the night.

"This is *not* what I came here for," she said more firmly.

Dake tucked a finger under her chin and raised her face until she was looking directly at him. "Then why did you come, Mel? To talk me out of a million dollars? I find that hard to believe."

She shrugged. "To find out why you'd left. To— Maybe so," she interrupted herself with a defiance she hardly felt. "Maybe that's exactly why."

Dake looked at her curiously. In the shadowy light his eyes shone bright and clear, like tiger eyes. His smile was almost gone.

"You thought you'd learn why I walked out, then decide how to bring me back into the fold?"

Melissa shrugged. She stepped around him, moved on beyond the bed toward the door, and picked up her coat from the chair where he had tossed it.

"Maybe," she muttered.

When Dake turned to face her, his hands were jammed into his back pockets. "And here I thought you were so careful about keeping your two lives separate."

Melissa looked at him sharply. She was absurdly conscious of his bare feet on the peach carpet, and of the way his jeans pulled across his thighs.

"If you're suggesting that that kiss was part of some plan, that's insulting!" she snapped. "Even if I *had* come here with some end in mind, it most certainly wouldn't have involved making a play for you. I didn't start this!"

Dake shrugged. "It wouldn't be the first time Ransom has dangled some bait in front of me that I couldn't refuse."

Melissa stared at him for a moment. Then she pulled the door open, stepped through it into the hallway, and slammed it shut behind her. So much for the silence of the night, she thought as she stalked down the hall to the elevator. Bob Rudge, much as she hated to admit it, was absolutely right on this one: Dakin Quarry was an arrogant, spoiled brat.

But her dreams that night were full of panthers and leopards pacing the African savannahs, of cougars racing across the western hills. In her dreams she could see the sleek muscles of their bodies, in movement and at rest, always ready, always alert. And in her dreams she wanted to touch the clean, lithe lines of their bodies. In spite of the danger.

- 3 -

MELISSA STRIPPED OFF her yellow jogging suit, gingerly
pulling it away from skin still damp and warm from her
morning run. She had come the long way around, by the
lake instead of through town, and the hypnotic blankness
of the water had helped clear her head of last night's
dreams. The Art Institute dinner seemed far, far away,
and room 1222 at the Palmer House even farther.

She smiled at her image in the mirror. It felt pleasantly
safe to be back in the office, back at work, after the
unexpected and disconcerting events of the evening before.

She toweled off, unfolded a plaid wool skirt and a
navy turtleneck sweater from her woven backpack, and
dressed quickly for work. As she hung the jogging jacket
and pants over a towel rack, she murmured a soft thank
you to the powers that be for her private bathroom.

Melissa settled comfortably into the big chair behind
her desk and plumped her backpack down beside her.
From its seemingly bottomless depths, she retrieved the
stack of pledge cards from last night's dinner and began
shuffling them into alphabetical order.

The door to her office creaked, and she looked up as a tousled head of red hair appeared around it.

"Boss? You free?"

Melissa leaned back in her chair and smiled. "Yep. You look tired, Jeffrey."

The young man who stepped into her office shook his head ruefully. "I'm *never* gonna get used to this eight-to-four stuff," he said. "How'd the dinner go?"

Melissa nodded. "Just fine." She riffled the pledge cards on her desk blotter. "Money, money, money," she said with a comic leer.

Jeff smiled, and his sleepy eyes seemed to gain a little energy. "Great. Sorry I couldn't make it. I would've been happy to come."

Melissa shook her head firmly. "Classes come first, Jeff. That was our deal."

"Well, if it weren't coming up on exams—"

"Exams or no exams," she interrupted, "that's your priority. You put in your eight hours a day." Melissa smiled. "I get my money's worth out of you, my boy. So what's up?"

Jeff ran a hand through his curls, succeeding only in making them more unruly. "Call from the prez."

"President Warren?" Melissa's eyes widened in surprise.

"The very same." Jeff nodded.

"At this hour? I just saw him last night."

Jeff shrugged and glanced at his watch. "He called precisely twenty minutes ago. Said he was sitting in his office reading the *Wall Street Journal* and he saw a name he'd heard last night. Dakin Quarry. Man makes jogging shoes."

Melissa felt her shoulders stiffen slightly at the name, and she folded her hands primly in her lap. She looked at Jeff quizzically. "And?"

Jeff glanced at the piece of paper in his hand. "Seems someone mentioned to him last night that Mr. Quarry had come and gone rather ... um ... *abruptly,* I think, was the word he used. At the dinner, that is. And now he's reading in the *Journal* that the man's shoes are the hottest things since Frisbees. So he wants to know what the story is."

Jeff stopped and smiled. His eyes were no longer sleepy. "So Dakin Quarry turned up, huh?" he added.

Melissa ducked her head. Sometimes it seemed as if Jeff were one step ahead of her, and she didn't want him reading any messages about Dakin Quarry on her face. She had hired this fresh Ransom graduate as her secretary after interviewing a dozen qualified applicants. He was bright, ambitious, and committed heart and soul to Ransom College. And despite the inconvenience of his continuing education—he was pursuing an M.A. in English down the road at Northwestern—and his frequent half-awake appearance, he was on top of everything. She had never regretted her decision.

"You expected him to, I take it?" she asked a little dryly.

Jeff shrugged. "I had a hunch. Nobody's gone after him for years, as far as I can see from the file. It was certainly worth sending out a second invitation."

Suddenly Jeff picked up one leg and propped a foot on Melissa's desk. She blinked. There it was, a powder-blue shoe with a golden lightning bolt down the side.

"*Every*body's buying his shoes," he said.

Melissa scowled and pushed his foot away. "Okay, you've made your point. Thank you for sending the second invitation. Yes, Dakin Quarry turned up at the dinner. Yes, he left early. No, I'm not sure why."

She paused for a moment and evened the edges of the stacked pledge cards. "But I'm going to find out," she continued more softly, "and when I do . . ."

Jeff held up both hands, palms forward. "The man had best watch out," he said, amused. "But don't tell me; tell the prez." He picked up the phone from her desk and punched several buttons, then handed Melissa the receiver. "Here you go." He smiled as Melissa exchanged pleasantries with the president of the college.

"Yes, sir, he was, and he did," Melissa responded to President Warren's question. "Yes, I'm aware that he's turned into quite a catch."

She listened for a moment as the president read from the newspaper article that was evidently in his hand.

"I certainly plan to find out why he left. He seems to harbor a certain amount of hostility..."

She paused again, listening to the voice booming over the line.

"Yes, sir. I'll get on it as soon as I can. But I think we need to know a lot more about him before we make any kind of approach. I need some time to get to know him." Suddenly Melissa could feel a warmth in her cheeks that reminded her of how close she had come to getting to know him very well indeed just a few hours earlier. "On paper, of course," she added weakly.

Melissa took a deep breath. "Yes, sir," she answered. "I'll make him a number-one priority. I'll do my best." She hung the phone up gently, then slapped the desk hard with her open palm.

Jeff looked at her curiously. "My, my," he said mildly.

Melissa glared. "I don't like being told how to do my job!" she said. But even as she heard her own words, she knew that was the least of it. President Warren was clearly right: Dake Quarry *should* be a target for Ransom's development office—*before* he ended up on the cover of *Time* and had everyone in the country hounding him for donations. But the man was *confusing*.

"The prez tends to have pretty good instincts," Jeff said.

Melissa sank back in her chair and let her body relax. "I know," she said. "He's good. And he believes in the same things I do, or I wouldn't have taken this job. But..."

Jeff smiled sleepily. "Yeah. But."

She pushed herself away from the desk and stood up.

"I suppose you know exactly what we have in our files?" she asked.

Jeff nodded. "Not much. Mostly the clippings I've found in the last couple of months. Something in *Business Week* in the middle of the summer mentioned he was from here, and then when his name turned up on one of our mailing-list printouts a month or so after that, I started watching for him in the papers."

He disappeared into his own office for a moment, then returned with a folder in his hand. "Hardly anything on the man himself," he said. "It's mostly about his company."

Melissa glanced through the articles Jeff handed her. As he had said, almost all of it focused on the innovative design of Windflame running shoes and the way the company had taken off suddenly the previous spring.

"How come nobody pointed him out to me as something special before now?"

Jeff shook his head. "He's not really. I mean, he's no richer than half the other alums from here. It's just that he's come into it rather quickly."

Melissa nodded slowly, still skimming the clippings. "Basically," she said after another moment, "we've really got nothing on this guy. So let's try to find something."

She sat down again and looked up at Jeff. "See if you can find his undergraduate file. And check the campus newspaper files for the years he was here. Let's see what kind of student he was."

She could hear the businesslike crispness in her voice, and she allowed herself a small smile. The reactions Dake Quarry produced in the pit of her stomach were hardly businesslike.

Jeff clicked his heels together and saluted. "Aye, aye, sir," he said solemnly, then spun around on the balls of his feet and left the room.

It was shortly before lunchtime when he reappeared clutching two manila folders.

"Speedy delivery," he said with a sweeping bow. He pushed the pile of pledge cards she was annotating aside and spread the folders out in front of her. "Undergraduate record, *Daily Collegian* articles," he added, pointing first at one file and then at the other.

Melissa nodded. Her palms felt suddenly damp, and she pulled a tissue from a pocket of her skirt and wiped them. She didn't feel quite ready to tackle Dakin Quarry yet.

"Well done. I'll get to them after lunch." She pushed the folders to one side of the desk and pulled the pledge cards back into the center.

Jeff frowned. "But don't you want to know——"

"I'll look at them after lunch," Melissa repeated, glancing up at her assistant with a coolness in her eyes that belied the warmth she was feeling elsewhere in her body. "Honest. Thanks, Jeff."

He shrugged and grinned. "Somehow I got the impression that Mr. Dakin Quarry was a hot subject around here."

Melissa blinked and quickly looked down at the pledge cards so Jeff wouldn't see the smile playing at her mouth. Hot indeed, she told herself wryly. Very hot.

"Well," she said, still looking at her desk, "he's a high priority. But we *do* have a few other things to get to, too. For instance, the Christmas cards." Melissa looked up pointedly at Jeff, and he shifted his weight from one foot to the other.

"Okay," he said grudgingly, clearly disappointed at being relegated to more computer-tending. "See you after lunch."

Melissa grinned and waved him back into his own office. She picked up the next pledge card in her pile and matched it with a card in the file on her desk, made a notation on each, then moved on to another. But her eyes shifted constantly to the files lying at the side of her desk.

Finally, with a sigh, she pulled one toward her and opened it. *Dear Dakin,* read the first letter in the folder, *We at Ransom College send you our congratulations on your state record . . .*

She heard the door to her office open again.

"Jeff—" she began, looking up.

But it wasn't a redheaded twenty-one-year-old who now stood peering around the door to her office. It was a very tall, very dark, very gorgeous man in his mid-thirties. Melissa swallowed a gulp.

"Dake," he corrected. "Dake Quarry."

"You!" she said. Suddenly aware of the open file in front of her, Melissa closed it and slid it quickly beneath the second one.

"Me. Your mouth is open."

Melissa snapped her mouth shut. Dake was smiling, and his eyes glittered with amusement. He was wearing faded jeans again, but the sports jacket had been replaced by a khaki windbreaker. Beneath it was a navy turtleneck sweater—a twin to her own. His thick dark hair fell back in soft wings away from his face.

"May I come in?" he asked, taking a cautious step into the office. "There wasn't anyone around out there, and—" He stopped mid-sentence. "Boy, you really are as beautiful as I remembered," he added softly.

Melissa rubbed her palms together in her lap. Pull yourself together, she commanded herself. And keep in mind that the president has ordered you to be nice to the man.

"It's only been twelve hours," she said dryly. "Of course, come in." Then she stood up, her professional smile in place. "This is unexpected."

She stepped around the side of her desk and held a hand out to him. He covered the distance between them in long, easy strides and shook her hand firmly.

"Glad we're still speaking," he said with a nod.

Memories of the night before flooded through Melissa, and she slid her hand out of his and tucked it deep into the side pocket of her skirt. Just hang on, Markham, she told herself. Just hang on.

"Of course." Her voice sounded tight and a little sulky to her own ears. "Giving Ransom another chance, are you?" she asked, this time self-consciously bright.

Dake ignored her question and glanced around the room instead. "Nice office," he said politely. "Quite nice."

He gazed out at the view of Ransom's central quadrangle and moved closer to the window. "I see the panther's still there."

He pointed to the statue of a panther about to spring—Ransom's mascot—in the middle of the quad. His voice sounded amused, and there was a vaguely curious expression on his face. "I always had a perverse kind of affection for that thing."

He continued to look out the window for a long moment, and when he turned back toward her, his eyes were thoughtful. Melissa, both hands safely in her pockets, watched him take a step toward her. His eyes were ebony, and some kind of power, a force field, seemed to radiate from them. She pulled one hand out and pressed it against the desk for support.

"Mel, I'm sorry about last night," he said finally. "I haven't gotten much in the way of sleep."

Melissa looked at him through slightly narrowed eyes. What was it about his calling her Mel that appealed to her so much? Last night she had felt some sense of equality, as though he was acknowledging her as a strong, independent being just by his choice of nickname. Today there was something else as well, some familiarity, that also appealed to her.

"I got just about all the way home," he went on, "this morning. Then I realized that all I was doing was thinking about you."

His eyes held hers for a moment longer, and then he shrugged and smiled. He looked out the window again. "You know, I haven't been back on this campus in fifteen years," he mused. "Thought I'd never set foot on it again." His gaze returned to Melissa, and his smile became a grin. "You must be pretty powerful stuff, Mel, to get me through those gates."

Melissa lowered her eyes to the desk. She felt a torrent of confusion, and the shiver of excitement Dake's presence caused was back again full force.

"So, I'm sorry," he finished up.

"Nothing to apologize for," Melissa muttered. "I . . . I had a little control problem last night myself."

Dake laughed, and Melissa ventured a smile.

"I seem to spend half my time apologizing to you," he observed. "I think the problem is context, pure and simple." He gestured toward the view out the window. "Seems I'm not as ready to deal with Ransom College again as I thought I was yesterday afternoon. We've got to get ourselves away from all this. Give ourselves a chance to figure out if this thing is . . ." He hesitated, then laughed again. "More than just lust," he concluded.

Melissa stared at him. "Lust?" she repeated coldly. "I must tell you that's not a sensation I'm in the habit of feeling."

Dake's eyes widened. "Funny," he said, "last night I would have sworn . . ." He left his words dangling in the air as Melissa's cheeks flushed Ransom red.

"Dake," she scolded, "please. Let's be serious. It seems we're going to be thrown together by my job in any case, and we're going to have to—"

"No seriousness allowed," he interrupted, waggling a finger at her. "Come on, Mel. It's a perfect day. Come have lunch with me, somewhere far, far away. I bet you haven't been out in the fresh air since eight this morning."

"I ran to work," she said quickly, a little defensively.

"Exactly," he said, pouncing on her words. "And now it's noon, and it's one of those incredible Chicago surprises: The sky is perfectly blue, and the lake is perfectly calm." Suddenly he moved a single step forward and took hold of her hand.

An astonishing ripple of desire ran through Melissa, starting in her fingers and ending somewhere deep inside. She clutched at the desk with her other hand.

"Come on," he said again. "We'll go for a drive along the lake, and we'll talk about you and me. No Ransom College. They owe you some hours off, after last night. Besides, it's Friday."

He looked at her beseechingly, his eyes wide and

innocent. Then one corner of his mouth tilted up in amusement. "Anyway, you might just slip in a question or two that would help with your job, and I'd hardly even notice."

In a way he was right, she knew: She *could* get some much-needed information just by talking with him. But if she accepted his invitation, she admitted sheepishly, that would hardly be the reason.

"I . . ." Melissa tipped her head to one side, uncertain.

Like a small boy, he pulled at her hand. "Come *on,* Mel. Give up!"

Melissa shook her head helplessly as Dake led her across the room toward the door. She snatched up her jacket from the coat rack in the outer office.

You are an idiot, she told herself as she pulled the door shut behind them. A world-class idiot. This man spells trouble in forty different ways, and you are not equipped to fend him off. But then, she added with a little smile, who wants to?

She shook her head. Cardinal rule of fund-raising, she argued with herself: No personal involvements. Keep it business, Markham. Just keep it business.

Dake opened the door of a sleek, dark green Fiat parked just outside the building—in a NO PARKING zone, Melissa noted ironically. Still Ransom's bad boy. She glanced at him as he started the engine. His straight hair hung just below the high neck of his sweater, and in profile his cheekbones seemed even higher, his eyes even more deep-set.

He concentrated on maneuvering the car through the campus, hardly glancing anywhere but straight ahead. Melissa had the distinct feeling he was trying not to see anything around him. His hands on the wheel were tense, the knuckles pale. It wasn't until they drove out through the big stone gate and headed for Lake Shore Drive that he visibly relaxed.

Dake was true to his word. They drove along the curving shore of Lake Michigan toward downtown in a

silence that felt comfortable. Melissa rested her head
back against the seat and looked at the view—all brilliant
blues and fluffy white clouds and glittering reflections
of the sun off glass skyscrapers.

"Where're you from, Mel?" Dake asked finally.

She sat up straight again. "Near Pittsburgh." She smiled
at the high-rise buildings to their right. "I remember when
I first saw Chicago. I don't know what I was expecting—
maybe another Pittsburgh. Something very dark and
heavy. But I think it was the sailboats on the lake that
really got to me. Anyway, it was love at first sight."

Dake nodded. "For me, too. I remember coming in
from the airport." He grinned. "I was terrified."

"I have trouble picturing you terrified of anything,"
Melissa said with a laugh.

Dake glanced at her. "Oh, yeah. I was your basic farm
boy," he said. "I'd only been out of Colorado once, for
the national junior championships, and we were pretty
much kept under lock and key there. Here was this city
so big you could see it for miles around. Not to mention
this hotshot college I was going to."

Dake guided the Fiat into an exit lane and off the
Drive. "I've been a lot of places since," he said, "but I
always seem to come back to Chicago."

"Ransom brought you here the first time," Melissa
said quietly. "That's something good the school did for
you. You wouldn't have discovered Chicago if you hadn't
been recruited."

Dake pulled into a parking place in the Lincoln Park
lot and switched off the ignition. He shifted against the
seat to look at her. He nodded, his expression thoughtful,
as though he were hearing something he knew but had
forgotten.

"Maybe," he said. "Maybe that's true."

They locked the car, put money into the meter, and
headed into the zoo. The sun was unusually warm for
mid-November. Chicago fall, Melissa thought—always
a time to be savored. Most of the zoo animals were

outside sunning themselves, taking full advantage of this last respite before winter's arrival.

Dake and Melissa trailed aimlessly among the cages and the newer, more open environments. They stopped wherever something caught their eyes, and now and again they talked.

"Now *that* looks familiar," Melissa laughed. They were leaning on a metal railing by the children's section, in front of a family of pigs.

Dake stared at her. "Pigs?" he asked incredulously. *"You're* familiar with *pigs?"*

Melissa nodded a little fiercely. "You're not the only farm kid around," she said. "My family kept sheep and pigs both."

He looked at her, dark eyebrows raised. "Your father farmed? I thought you said you lived in Pittsburgh."

Melissa shook her head. *"Near* Pittsburgh," she said. "Northeast. We lived on a farm." She paused for a moment. "But my father wasn't a farmer. He was a lawyer, actually."

"Ah." Dake turned toward the pigs again.

"And a judge," she murmured. Why did she feel so defensive? Nothing wrong with lawyers and judges.

"My mother weaves," she added. "And spins her own wool. I helped take care of the animals."

"Of course," Dake said finally.

"What's that supposed to mean?" she asked, shifting against the railing to face him.

Dake shrugged. His shoulders strained against the light fabric of his tan windbreaker, and she sucked in her breath a little.

"You," he said flatly, "are like everybody else who went to Ransom College."

Her eyes widened a little. "And what," she repeated, "does *that* mean?" Her voice was quieter now, more self-assured. She could defend herself against that kind of stupid generalization.

Dake leaned sideways against the railing and looked

at her. The blue of the sky and the lake made an almost painful brightness behind him, and Melissa raised a hand to shield her eyes.

"Well-to-do," he said with another shrug. His head was tilted back, giving the familiar hooded look to his eyes, but there was no hint of the sudden iciness she had seen in them before. "Unconcerned. Smart but not wise."

"That's not fair," she answered quickly. "That's a generalization, and it doesn't hold water. Just because I could pay my own way through college doesn't mean I was unaware that other people couldn't."

"Ah, yes. That's right. You were little-miss-concerned-with-the-world's-problems, weren't you? Even married a doctor to help make things better."

Melissa blinked at the cruelty of Dake's words. "That's not fair," she repeated. "You make it sound as if . . ." She hesitated, then plunged on as anger took control. "You seem to feel you have some kind of corner on compassion, Dake. Well, you sound like an arrogant prig. I've spent half my life raising money for good causes. Where do you get off sounding holier-than-thou just because you had to go through college on a scholarship? Bob Rudge said you were a spoiled brat, and I'm beginning to think it's true."

Melissa saw Dake's body stiffen until every line of it looked hard. She felt a tiny jolt of fear deep inside. Now you've done it, she told herself. Now you've gone too far.

She raised a hand to her hair and pushed it back with an uncertain gesture. "Dake," she said, "I'm sorry. I really am. I didn't mean . . . I just can't seem to stay in control around you."

His shoulders relaxed perceptibly, but his features were still harsh as he studied the family of pigs in silent concentration.

Melissa took a deep breath. "Look, Dake," she went on, "obviously you had a bad experience at Ransom. If we're going to be . . . If we're going to see each other, we can't just ignore that. Not with the job I have. You've got to tell me about it."

Dake looked at her steadily for a moment. His hair blew over his forehead, and he pushed it back with that oddly appealing gesture. His expression softened, and he smiled just a little. Melissa moistened her dry lips with the tip of her tongue.

"Okay," he said. "Fair enough. Let's get a hot dog."

They stood silently in line, then took their hot dogs and coffee to an empty bench. Melissa put her cup down carefully between them.

Dake sat sideways on the bench, looking at her. "Okay," he began. "You've no doubt read the college file on me, but I'll go over the ground again for you."

Melissa started to contradict him, then thought better of it and sat silently.

"Bob Rudge approached me at the state track championships in Boulder. I'd had letters from lots of places by then, including Ransom, because I already held the national record in the four-forty. But he actually turned up at the meet. That impressed me."

Dake took a bite of his hot dog and chewed it slowly. He was looking over Melissa's shoulder, as if at something in the distance, and his eyes were thoughtful.

"I played basketball, too," he continued after a moment, "and I was planning to play basketball in college, because I figured there was better money in that afterward. But Rudge wanted me for his track team. I knew Ransom had a good team. I also knew it was a first-class college academically. I wanted a good education. It was very important to my parents, too. So we came to an agreement."

He took another big bite of his hot dog and a swallow of coffee. Melissa sipped hers, keeping her eyes on his face.

"I won a lot of races for Ransom the first two years, but there were some problems with the deal, as far as I was concerned. I had to live in a special dorm with the other scholarship athletes. And there was a lot of pressure to take certain courses, where professors were cozy with athletes. I'd come to Ransom for an education. I wasn't interested in that kind of game."

Melissa frowned. "That's crazy," she said flatly. "I don't remember that kind of thing happening."

"How many scholarship athletes did you know?" Dake challenged.

She thought for a moment. "I went out with a guy for a while who played basketball. He . . ." Her frown deepened. "He lived at the dorm up by the field house, but that was just because he had to eat at the training table every night."

Dake nodded. "And so that the coaching staff could keep a careful eye on their investment."

"Well," Melissa said doubtfully, "that makes a certain amount of sense."

Dake shook his head sharply. "Why? I was holding up my end of the bargain. I was performing for Ransom College. But Ransom wanted me in some special little cubbyhole. We were monkeys on strings, Melissa. Just performing monkeys. If we'd been female, the women's movement would have made us a prime cause."

Melissa shook her head stubbornly. "Well, I'm sorry that happened. But you *did* get a free education."

"Not quite," Dake answered quietly. "The problem with a dancing monkey is, if you can't dance anymore, they cut the string and leave you out there on your own."

His dark eyes were cloudy, and he was silent for a moment, almost as if he were composing himself against his own anger. When he spoke again, his tone was cooler, a little distant.

"I had the bad taste to get hurt the fall of my junior year. Tore an Achilles tendon during hurdles practice a few weeks before the indoor season started. Our Mr. Rudge told me to run in the first meet anyway. I tore the tendon again. I said no more races, at least until the following fall, and they said okay, no more money. Period."

Dake stood up and held out a hand to Melissa.

"Enough," he said. "Let's go see the hippos. They've always been my favorites."

She folded her arms in front of her. "No," she said. "That's not right. They took your scholarship away because you'd gotten hurt? Or because you refused to compete?"

Dake shrugged and jammed his hands into the pockets of his windbreaker. "It doesn't really matter, does it? Either way, I was out of funds."

Melissa shook her head. "But it *does* matter. If it was because you got hurt, that's simply wrong. It's not the athlete's fault if he's injured. But if it was because you wouldn't run once you were healed . . ."

She picked up her coffee and sipped the last of it, then carefully tucked her napkin into it. "Why wouldn't you compete?"

"Because, dear lady, I might be walking around with a limp right now if I had." He bent over and leaned on an imaginary cane.

"Is that what the doctors said?"

Dake drew in a deep breath and let it out slowly. Then he sat down again beside her, sweeping the trash from his own lunch to the end of the bench.

"You're a stubborn one, Mel," he said. "Okay. A doctor I trusted said that. It was *my* damn leg, after all. And now, fifteen years later, you wouldn't get any argument at all on it. In fact, it's likely I'd have surgery for the same injury."

"Well, then, why would Rudge make you run?" Melissa asked.

Dake picked up a napkin and folded it into a tiny square. "Unfortunately, Coach Rudge listened to a different doctor. *His* doctor said a couple of weeks' rest was all a torn tendon needed—that and a few shots of painkiller." He shrugged. "I was only twenty years old; I tried it their way once. When it tore again, I said no deal. No more for a full year."

Melissa looked at him—at the soft darkness of his

eyes and the high, sharp curves of his cheekbones; at the smooth, easy lines of his hair, ruffled now by the wind; at the full sensuality of his mouth. She wanted to believe him; she wanted it desperately. But Rudge had coached for more years than Dake had run—wouldn't he understand injuries? And Dake had refused to compete, refused to do what he had agreed to do when he had accepted Ransom's offer of an education.

"Melissa," Dake said softly, responding to the obvious confusion in her expression, "you can't understand what it's like—the pressure that's put on you. I was bucking a very popular system, and I had only myself to decide what was best. No lawyer father to come to my rescue. What these people were asking me to do was to risk permanent injury so they could take home a trophy from some damn track meet."

Melissa fiddled with the cup in her hand, pulling the edge of the napkin above its rim and then pushing it down inside again. After a moment, Dake impatiently took it out of her hand. He rose, picked up his own cup and napkin, and tossed everything into a trash basket at the other side of the broad walkway. Then he came back and sat down again.

"Melissa . . ." He lifted one hand to her face and touched her cheek lightly. "My beautiful Alice in Wonderland. Look around you. Try to see the real world."

She felt the warmth of his hand against her cheek, cold now from the lake wind. He rested his other hand gently on her knee, turning against the bench until he faced her directly. Melissa's gaze skimmed over his broad chest and wide shoulders, covered by the zipped-up windbreaker, then settled on his face. Tentatively, she reached out a hand and touched his hair. It was soft, as she had imagined it. She spread her fingers and ran them through its softness, as she had seen him do so often.

Dake brought his face closer to hers, and she felt the churning inside, the urgent stirring of desire. If she kissed him, she knew she'd be lost.

She pulled back from him.

"So they took your scholarship away," she said hoarsely. "And you had to work for a year and a half to pay your way through college. Or go to your parents for help. Lots of students do that. I don't see that it's worth fifteen years of bitterness."

Dake stared at her briefly, his fingers still against her cheek, then pulled his hand away. His body collapsed against the bench.

"Geez, Mel, give me a break here," he said plaintively. He scooted down a few inches on the bench, putting distance between them. "I thought the deal was that we weren't going to talk about Ransom. Haven't I given you enough?"

Melissa brushed a crumb off her skirt and stood up.

"Maybe that just won't work," she said. "You're talking about my being Alice. Seems to me it's *you* who's trying to live in Wonderland all the time." She put her hands into the pockets of her jacket. "Ransom College exists, Dake, whether you like it or not. You're going to have to acknowledge that sometime."

Dake looked up at her. He was slouched on the bench, hands in the pockets of his khaki jacket, one ankle resting on the other knee. A breeze caught his hair, and Melissa fought an almost overwhelming need to brush it into place again with her hand. She took a step back.

"Okay," he said finally, unfolding his long body from the bench. "This isn't gonna work. Let's go home."

They drove back to Ransom, and this time the silence was uncomfortable. Dake pulled the Fiat into the parking lot behind the administration building and switched off the ignition.

"I guess," he said, "you can take the girl out of the college, but you can't take the college . . . and so on."

Melissa clicked open the door. "Thanks for the afternoon," she said uncertainly, climbing out of the car. "I always like the zoo. I wish . . ." She hesitated.

Dake gave an ironic nod. "Me, too, Mel. I wish, too."

Melissa looked at him curiously through the open door. If only he weren't so damn handsome, she thought impatiently, this whole thing would be a lot easier.

"By the way," he said suddenly, leaning toward the door, "for what it's worth, I never took those recommended courses. I took what I wanted to take. And I learned a lot of good stuff here. I have to admit that."

He reached over and took hold of the door handle. With a smile that seemed to wrench the stability from Melissa's legs, he pulled the door shut. "Thanks for your company," he called, his voice barely audible through the closed door. "Maybe I'll see you around sometime."

The engine started up, and he backed the car away. Melissa stood for a moment, watching. Then she turned and went back to her office.

- 4 -

MELISSA RAN SIX miles on Saturday, four more on Sunday, and at eleven o'clock Sunday night she cleaned her apartment from top to bottom. By Monday morning she felt refreshed, as though she had shaken Dake Quarry's unsettling influence off her shoulders. She was ready to confront him again, at least on paper.

She gave a quick wave to Jeff as she passed through his office to her own. He trailed after her.

"Good weekend?" he asked casually, the door still open behind him.

Melissa nodded. "Mmm. Lots of exercise."

Jeff smiled. "You need some new running shoes," he said with a pointed glance at the very old, very shabby sneakers on her feet. Melissa kicked them off, pulled black pumps out of her backpack, and slipped into them. She had worn corduroy slacks and a burgundy sweater to work today, and she had bicycled instead of running.

"You oughta try Windflame Runners," Jeff added with a wicked grin.

Melissa made a face at him. "When I come into my inheritance," she said, "I'll buy some new shoes."

She settled at her desk.

"I went through Quarry's newspaper clippings," Jeff

said sleepily. "On Friday. When you were out of the office."

Melissa opened the top file and looked up at him. "And?"

"Where were you, anyway?" he asked.

Melissa looked at him silently for a moment. "What's in the file?" she asked finally, her voice steady.

He shrugged. "Starts mostly with sports. He won a whole lot of races his freshman and sophomore years. Elected co-captain of the team his second semester here, which is almost unheard of. Also apparently feuded with the coach some, right from the start. Carried on kind of low-key crusades against restricted course offerings and separate housing for scholarship athletes."

Melissa looked at him with a frown. "All that's in here?" she asked.

Jeff nodded. "Of course, the times were a tad tumultuous, and low-key crusades tended to get lost in the face of more world-shattering issues. But it's all there."

"Think I might have a chance to read it for myself?" Melissa asked pointedly.

She glanced down at the file for the first time, and Dakin Quarry's face stared up at her from it. She inhaled sharply. He looked very much the same—as much as she could tell from a grainy black-and-white photo—although there was a grin on his face that was more innocent and playful than any expression she had yet seen there. She was amused to see that his hair, just a little longer than the fashion now, had been precisely the same length then—just a little shorter than the fashion. Clearly, even then, Dake Quarry had marched to the sound of his own drummer.

Melissa smiled at the picture and let the warmth of looking at Dake move slowly through her. There was no denying it; she liked looking at him.

Jeff cleared his throat, and Melissa looked up abruptly. "Still here?" she asked.

"There's an interesting little item halfway through or

so. You ever hear the story of the guys who put the panther in a cage?"

"Sure," she said. "It's legend." She gestured toward the statue of the panther on the main quad, visible out her window. "They built a whole thing, with metal bars and everything. Took two days to get it down."

"That was Dake Quarry."

Melissa felt her smile become a grin. "No kidding." No wonder he had looked out at the panther on Friday with such a mixture of amusement and rue.

Jeff nodded. "A bunch of the guys from the track team. But he was the only one reprimanded in writing for it. They used that later, when they took his scholarship away, as evidence of his irresponsibility."

The grin faded. "Did they really?" she asked softly. "What happened to the other guys?"

"Nothing. Not so far as I could find, anyway."

There was a knock on the partially open door, and Melissa looked up to see Robert Rudge's florid face poking around it.

"Morning, darlin'," he said with a grin. "Mind if I come in for a minute?"

Melissa exchanged a quick glance with Jeff, then formed a cordial smile for Rudge.

"Of course not, Bob," she answered quickly before her instinctive dislike of him had time to move in. "Have a seat."

Bob Rudge breathed heavily as he rolled across the room and lowered his bulk into the comfortable chair across from Melissa's desk. Jeff gave them both a quick salute and disappeared into his office, closing the door behind him.

"Nice weekend?" Rudge asked genially.

Melissa nodded. "Yes, thanks." She closed the folder of Dake Quarry's press clippings carefully and gestured at the stack of pledge cards still sitting to one side of her desk. "I'm just trying to catch up from the dinner at the Art Institute."

Rudge nodded in return. "Busy time for us all. I won't keep you," he said. He breathed deeply, and a wheezy noise filled the office.

Melissa looked at him with slightly raised eyebrows. "Yes?" she asked.

He was silent for a moment until his labored breathing settled somewhat.

"Thought I might be of some help, ma'am," he said finally.

Melissa picked up a pencil and tapped it impatiently against Dake's folder. She was eager to read through it herself, to try to get a feel for what kind of person Dake had been at Ransom. To try to get to know him better.

"How so?" she asked when Rudge didn't go on.

Rudge nodded. "I hear on the grapevine that Jack Warren wants you to make Mr. Dakin Quarry number one on the hit list."

Melissa recoiled imperceptibly at the terminology. *Hit list* was not the way she looked at potential donors— although she did use the word *target,* she had to admit.

"Yes," she said again, her voice flat.

Rudge shrugged one shoulder. It made him look vaguely like a hippopotamus coming up for air. "Well, I thought maybe I could help."

Melissa rested her hand on the file folder of newspaper clippings.

"Actually," she said, "I had the impression that you and Dake Quarry weren't exactly best buddies. I'm not sure how you could—"

Rudge waved a pudgy hand in the air, then settled the sausagelike fingers back on the arm of his chair. "That was then," he said, grinning again. "Now is now."

Melissa looked at him, covering her distaste with a polite smile. "There didn't seem to be much love lost between you two the other night, either," she responded.

"We're not talkin' love, darlin', we're talkin' business," the coach explained. "Yes, sir, Mr. Dake Quarry is a businessman now, and if there's one thing I know about, it's business."

"I thought your area of expertise was sports," Melissa said dryly. Watch it, Markham, she told herself. Don't step on toes here.

"Sports *is* business, missy," Coach Rudge answered, sounding not the least offended. "That's my point." He smiled broadly. "And what I've got to offer Mr. Quarry is a nice fat freshman class of runners who're all gonna need shoes. Now, I have considerable say in where they purchase those shoes. And I'm thinkin' we might provide a little bait for Mr. Quarry, if you catch my meaning."

Melissa looked down at the folder on her desk and opened it, thumbing through it absently without really seeing anything except the picture of Dake. She didn't want to look up at Rudge again until the dislike she could no longer repress had faded from her expression.

But Rudge wasn't waiting for an answer.

"The thing is," he went on, "we have another kind of bait here to offer, too."

Melissa glanced up at him, and he winked broadly at her. "Some things never change, you know, darlin'. Quarry was always a skirt-chaser in college. Now, you, you got some very nice ammunition right there." He nodded toward her.

Melissa stared at him. "I don't think I understand," she said coolly.

Rudge winked again, the heavy flesh of his eyelid meeting the heavy flesh of his cheek like two fish kissing. Then he let his gaze meander slowly downward from Melissa's face to the outline of her breasts against the soft wool of her sweater.

"Oh, darlin'," he said, the wheeziness returning to his voice, "you got a whole lot more equipment for reeling in Dake Quarry than the man that sat in that seat before you had. You just need to use it."

Melissa stood up and folded her arms in front of her. She tried very hard to smile, but she wasn't at all sure she was being successful.

"Bob, I'm afraid I have different ideas about how to do my job than you have. I appreciate your interest in all this, but I just don't work that way."

Rudge waved a hand in the air. "Everybody works that way, darlin'. You better join on in."

Whatever smile had been on her face vanished. "I'm sorry, Bob. If I can't raise money for Ransom on its own merits, then it's not worth raising money for. Now if you'll excuse me..."

Rudge put both hands on the arms of his chair and pushed himself up. His red and white football jacket with *Coach Rudge* in script across the left pocket seemed to strain with the effort as he balanced himself.

"You have it your way, Miss Melissa. Just thought I might give you a couple of hints."

Melissa forced the smile back and unfolded her arms. "Thanks again for your interest, Bob."

He nodded. "Okay. I surely wouldn't want to keep you from your work." He winked again, then turned and pushed his way out through the door.

Melissa looked after him for a moment, her hands clenched into tight fists at her sides. She was still standing, staring at the door, when it opened again and Jeff's gentle face appeared around it.

"Boss?" he murmured. "Ready for company yet?"

Melissa blinked and unclenched her fists, then laughed. She shook her head. "I tell you, Jeff, I'm not sure what it is about that man..."

Jeff nodded vigorously. "I know. He affects me the same way. But I think we're in a distinct minority. Everybody else around here seems to think he's some kind of saint."

Melissa felt her body relax a little as she settled back into her chair. The *nerve* of him, to suggest first that they offer Quarry what amounted to a bribe in the form of business in return for his donation—and then to suggest that...

She shook her head sharply. It was, once again, that thin line. She was willing to flutter her eyelashes at some old goat if that's what made him happy; maybe that was all Rudge was suggesting she do for Dake Quarry. Why did she assume he meant anything more? Was it because she *wanted* more from Dake—wanted everything he had to give, and then some?

She took a deep breath to clear her head. "So, what's new?" she asked.

Jeff held out a slip of paper. "Alan McAllister just called. Can't come to the tailgate party and the game next Saturday."

Melissa reached for the message and skimmed it. "Hmm. That's too bad. He's such a spark plug at these things. And I have a couple of new people coming, too."

She mentally ran through the list of the twenty or so important alumni who had been invited to a pre-game party with the president and who would then be provided with the best seats in the stadium. She had organized three or four of these events, and the guest list changed slightly each time, but Alan McAllister was almost always included.

Now there was a place open for the following week, the Saturday after Thanksgiving.

Jeff shifted his weight from one foot to the other and cleared his throat. Melissa looked at him.

"You're allowed to say, 'I have an idea,'" she said with a smile.

He grinned. "I have an idea," he said.

Melissa nodded. "Out with it."

"How about inviting Dake Quarry?"

Melissa blinked. "Dake Quarry, Dake Quarry—all I hear about around here anymore is Dake Quarry! First President Warren, then Bob Rudge, and now you."

Jeff put his hands on his hips. "Well, it was just an idea."

"Mmm." She looked down at the folder on her desk. The thought of actually seeing Dake again—in the flesh—within the week made her stomach do somersaults. But it would be business, strictly business. Probably he wouldn't come—she was patently aware that he wasn't much interested in her business. Still, if she could coax him out, he would meet the president, and maybe Warren's office could take over the hunt altogether.

"Actually, it's a good idea," she said.

Jeff held out another slip of paper. "I just happen to have the phone number for Windflame Runners right here."

Laughing, Melissa snatched the paper from his hand. "Always prepared."

He saluted, three fingers raised to his forehead. "Always," he agreed.

She waited for Jeff to leave the office before dialing the number. The man who answered put her on hold briefly, and she was amused to hear Creedence Clearwater Revival—a favorite from her college days—rather than the usual unappetizing, unidentifiable background music.

It was only a matter of seconds before Dake's deep voice said hello.

"Dake," she said tentatively, "it's Melissa. Melissa Markham," she added quickly, fearful of presuming too much.

Dake laughed. "As opposed to the seven other Melissas I know," he said. "Hey, Mel, couldn't stay away from me?"

Melissa tried to keep the smile out of her voice. "Actually, this is more in the way of a business call," she said. "Or sort of a mix of business and pleasure. Maybe."

You're coming off like a real idiot, Markham, she chided herself. Just let your automatic pilot take over.

"How so?" Dake sounded suddenly wary and just a little distant.

"Well." Melissa cleared her throat. "We're having a small reception next Saturday—very small, just a handful of distinguished alumni, actually—before the football game. President Warren would like to invite you as his guest. To the reception. And to the game, too."

"Distinguished alumni?" Dake repeated. Melissa

wished she could see his face, see if the glimmer in his dark eyes was there, or if the icy sharpness she had seen once or twice before had taken over again. His voice was cool and neutral.

She took a deep breath and blew it out quickly to steady herself. "Come on, Dake, give me a break. I'm inviting you to meet the president. And I'm offering you a ticket to a football game that's been sold out for a week. How about it?"

"I hate football."

Melissa heard the hint of a western drawl in the way he drew out *hate*. His voice no longer sounded distant.

"So do I," she agreed sincerely. "But I'd—" She stopped. I'd like to see you again, she had been about to say.

"You'd what?" He sounded as if he was about to laugh.

"I'm willing to go if you are," she said. "Deal?"

There was a tiny pause.

"Tell you what, Mel. I'll try. It's busy here like you wouldn't believe. Christmas and all. But I'll think over your proposal, and I'll see what I can do. Fair?"

Melissa nodded. "Okay," she agreed. "It *is* short notice. If you can make it, we'll be meeting at the south end of the parking lot outside the stadium. About twelve."

There was another brief pause, and then Dake exploded in laughter. It was a deep, rich laughter that echoed over the phone line.

"You're talking about a *tailgate* party? This elegant reception with the president?"

"Yeah." She could feel the flush in her cheeks. "I guess I made it sound like something a little more refined."

"You sure did, Mel. But I'll keep it in mind, anyway. Twelve o'clock, in the parking lot. Wear a red carnation, so if I come, I'll know which one you are."

Then, without even a good-bye, he hung up.

Melissa stared at the receiver for a moment longer. He hadn't said he'd come, but he hadn't said he wouldn't.

And she wasn't at all certain which she wanted him to do.

The week seemed particularly busy because of the holiday on Thursday, since five days of work had to be crammed into three. Melissa spent most of her time over-seeing the Christmas mailing and wishing that the computer system for her office were entirely on line. Until then, projects like this had to be checked by her own reliable eyes.

On Wednesday evening, with a feeling of relief, Melissa watched the first batch of Christmas cards get packed up for the mailroom. On Thursday she shared a relaxed Thanksgiving with the McAllisters.

They sat back in their chairs in the late afternoon, the remnants of a twenty-pound turkey still on the sideboard, and sipped coffee. Melissa made occasional forays into her pumpkin pie, and Katherine smiled at her.

"It's certainly nice to have you here, Lissie," she said, "with the girls off, and only Tony around out of our three." She nodded toward the living room, where the McAllisters' twenty-three-year-old son sat watching a football game, his arm around his girl friend.

Melissa nodded. "It's nice for me, too. Having a sur-rogate family. Not to mention the fact that it sets my mom's mind at ease. If it weren't for you folks, she'd assume I was eating beans out of a can and going to a movie by myself on Thanksgiving. She believes in big family holidays. She can't quite grasp the idea of my being alone and liking it."

Katherine nodded firmly. "I agree with her," she said. Alan came back from the kitchen with another pot of coffee.

"By the way, Melissa, I'm sorry about Saturday," he said. "Anyone using my ticket?"

Melissa suddenly realized that they hadn't talked about Ransom virtually all day. An awareness of Dake flooded through her, of his need to avoid Ransom. Maybe it *was* possible . . .

She looked at Alan. "Maybe," she answered cautiously. "I . . . I asked Dakin Quarry if he'd be interested. You met him at the dinner last week."

Katherine leaned forward suddenly. "That man who walked out? Oh, Melissa, he was *so* attractive!"

Melissa nodded, and Alan chuckled softly. "My wife the matchmaker," he said.

Melissa's hand trembled suddenly, and she spilled a little coffee over into the saucer of her cup.

"What happened with him, anyway?" Katherine asked, ignoring Alan's comment. "Oh! I remember, there was that note . . ." She stopped and looked mischievously at Melissa. "What did happen, Lissie?"

Melissa shrugged. "Nothing." Well, it's the truth, she told herself defiantly. "Nothing at all. But President Warren has decided Dake needs to be cultivated, so Jeff suggested we offer him Alan's place at the tailgate party."

Alan nodded thoughtfully. "He seemed like an interesting man," he said. "I remember vaguely when he was at college. He was one terrific runner. I'd like to see him again sometime. Away from all that Ransom claptrap."

Katherine looked shocked. "Claptrap?" she asked.

Alan smiled. "Oh, no offense, darling. You know my feelings about Ransom. But I had the sense that Quarry would come off a lot better away from all that. There was sure *something* he resented."

Melissa nodded. "Maybe so. But my job is to get him right back into the middle of it, claptrap and all."

Katherine reached across the table and patted her hand. "Don't you pay any attention to Alan, Lissie. He's just mad because he has to go out of town. *He* wants to be at that football game on Saturday himself."

Melissa smiled, but the question of whether or not Dake Quarry would appear two days later had taken over the forefront of her mind. She helped Katherine stack dishes in the dishwasher, then took leave of the McAllisters.

That night she dreamed of a huge black panther, waiting for her, tracking her, always ready to spring. And she wanted only to put a cage around it and keep it as her very own, for ever and ever.

On Saturday morning, with trembling hands, she pulled on tan corduroy slacks and a cotton turtleneck. Impatiently, she added a thick Irish-knit sweater, wrapped a Ransom red and white muffler around her neck, then stepped into leather boots and headed downstairs.

Some part of her didn't want to leave her apartment. The second floor of an old house, it was comfortable and cozy, with thrift-shop treasures in every nook and cranny. What part of her really wanted to do was to curl up under the down quilt on her bed and leave the football game to the others. With a sigh, she stepped out onto the porch and locked the door.

The small northern Chicago suburb that was home to Ransom College was already beginning to fill with traffic. Football was a big event here, partly because so many alumni lived in the Chicago area. The team could always count on a good turnout.

At the edge of campus, students in sandwich boards were hawking banners and horns and big Ransom-red carnations. Melissa smiled and gave a wave, then stopped suddenly. Why not? she asked herself with a little thrust of her chin. She pulled a five-dollar bill out of her floppy shoulder bag and handed it to the boy with the carnations.

With the big red flower pinned securely to one shoulder, Melissa strode happily on toward the stadium.

But Dake Quarry wasn't there. At least he wasn't among the half-dozen VIPs who were mingling in the roped-off area of the parking lot. And he didn't appear as she checked over the metal tables, covered with white paper tablecloths, that held the buffet of barbecued beef on rolls, potato salad, sliced ham, and lots of beer.

It was almost half an hour later, in fact, when the parking lot was almost full and dozens of tailgate picnics were in loud progress, that Melissa caught sight of his tall figure out of the corner of her eye. He was making his way through the parked cars; he wore the usual faded jeans and a dark brown leather flight jacket with fur around the collar.

She finished her sentence, then excused herself and headed for the opening in the ropes that marked the entrance.

Dake was smiling.

"Hey, Mel!" he called when he got within calling distance. "Nice little crowd." He waved a hand, letting his broad gesture take in the noisy, animated group inside the ropes as well as the lot full of cars and people outside.

He came to a stop in front of her, and Melissa felt the familiar shiver run through her as he patted her arm with one hand. His dark eyes glimmered in the bright afternoon sun, and his bronze cheeks were touched with red by the sharp, tingly fall wind. Melissa knew that by late afternoon they would need the extra blankets she had already stowed under the bleachers by President Warren's seat.

She could see, up close, that the leather jacket was cracked and worn; it also looked immensely comfortable. Melissa swallowed hard.

"Glad you could make it," she said, her voice loud above the noise of the crowd. "I'd about given up on you."

His smile broadened, and he lifted one hand and touched the red carnation. "But you wore your red flower," he said softly. Melissa had to lean her head toward him to catch the words, and she could feel the strength of his hand, resting now against her shoulder.

"And you dressed formally, too," she said sardonically with a pointed glance at his jeans.

His eyebrows rose. "You expected more for a football game?" he asked incredulously.

Melissa shrugged. "Come on in."

Dake let his hand remain for a moment longer, then took it away and stepped inside the ropes.

"Does this mean Ransom officially acknowledges me?"

he asked. His mouth was tilted into a half-smile.

Melissa leaned toward him again so she wouldn't have to shout. "Of course Ransom acknowledges you. Why not? Just because you pulled some pranks?"

Dake shrugged. "Because I never graduated," he said easily. Then his head rose and he looked around curiously. "I smell food," he added, and he headed for the buffet table, his long strides cutting across the crowded pavement like a cheetah's through thick-grown savannah grass.

Confused, Melissa watched him leave her behind. Then she felt a tug on her arm and had to turn to talk to another of her professional targets.

For the next half hour, she kept track of Dake, who was always, it seemed, one conversation away from her. Whenever she made an effort to move subtly to his side, he just as subtly moved away. But it was clear that he was being perfectly charming; people were talking about him, and President Warren caught Melissa's arm to tell her how pleased he was that she had reeled in Dakin Quarry. His words made her think of Coach Rudge— happily otherwise occupied with the game today.

"I really haven't figured out an approach," she began.

The president patted her arm. "Terrific job, Melissa, just terrific," he said and turned away.

It was almost time for Melissa to begin shepherding the alumni into the game when Dake slipped up beside her and stood close enough to make her feel the heat of him through her thick sweater. He leaned down, his mouth just grazing her hair.

"How'm I doing?" he whispered. "Making a hit?"

Melissa was listening to a more or less drunk but very rich alumnus tell her why she should keep a dog. She glanced at Dake but said nothing.

At the first break in the lecture on pets, she looked pointedly at her watch. "Well, if we're going to make kickoff, we'd better be getting inside." She smiled brightly at the man opposite, then at Dake. "Section C, the second box up. You'll see the red flags at the corners."

Then she leaned a little toward Dake as the dog man headed unsteadily toward the stadium. "You're doing very well indeed," she whispered, "from what I hear."

Dake raised a hand to his forehead in a mock salute and turned away. Melissa made her way through the group, shooing everyone on into the stadium. The parking lot was emptying quickly.

She waited until the last of her charges was on the way, checked with the caterers to make sure she was no longer needed, then started into the stands herself. Dake was nowhere to be seen—gone in with the rest of them, presumably. She felt a stab of annoyance. It wasn't that she didn't want Dake to fit in; she *did*. But still, he was paying so little attention to her.

Melissa smiled at her own mental ramblings. Markham, she told herself, you don't know *what* the hell you want from this guy. For once he's sticking to business. You should just do the same thing.

She headed into the stadium at Gate C and hesitated for a moment to let her eyes grow accustomed to the darkness under the stands. The noise from the crowds overhead sounded like some distant thundering herd of mammoths—a low, ceaseless roar punctuated by an occasional trumpeting sound.

The stairway up into the stands was straight ahead, and except for a few stragglers, the dark area around it was deserted. Melissa put one foot on the first step, then jumped and squeaked in fright as a hand grasped her arm.

She whirled around.

Dake was standing in the shadowy darkness beside the stairs.

"Sorry," he said softly. "Didn't mean to scare you." He smiled, and the whiteness of his teeth seemed to float in the air. His brown pilot's jacket and faded jeans, his bronze skin and black hair, all faded into the depths of shadow.

"The Cheshire Cat," Melissa whispered. Then she laughed in relief. She stepped down again. "I thought you'd gone on with the others," she said.

Her eyes had grown more used to the dimness. She could see the outline of his body clearly and could even make out his handsome features.

He shook his head. "Nope. I hate football."

His hand was still on her arm, and he raised the other to her shoulder and rested it there, just above the red carnation. Melissa felt the stirrings deep in her center that his touch provoked. She ran her tongue over her lips.

"So do you," Dake said. "You told me so."

Melissa nodded dumbly. "But—"

"And I've done my part," he went on. "I've performed perfectly. I was nice to everyone. Now I want my reward."

He moved closer, and Melissa felt the world begin to spin around her. She stepped abruptly backward, bumped into the metal railing of the stairway, and leaned gratefully against it for support.

"Is that how you think all this operates?" she said sharply. His face seemed blurred suddenly; everything seemed confused. "You do this for me, and then you get what you want in return? You think everything can be bought?"

Dake shook his head thoughtfully. "No, not bought. Earned. I perform; you pay. That's the way my contract with Ransom worked before."

Melissa held on to the railing with shaking fingers. Dake's hands were still on her shoulders, and now he began rubbing softly with them, making small circles Melissa could feel through her sweater.

"No," he said again. "I'm sorry, Mel. I don't mean that."

His hands were stronger now, the circles more sensual as he rubbed her shoulders.

"I learned a lesson here," he said softly. "At Ransom. And I'm afraid I haven't forgotten it." He hesitated a moment, and Melissa looked at his face. Instinctively, she took her hands from the railing and put them on his waist. "Help me forget it, Mel," he whispered. "Help me understand that people can trust each other, and—"

Melissa's lips parted just a little, and Dake leaned toward her. Then his mouth pressed against hers, and his hands tightened on her shoulders. He pulled her to him, and Melissa felt the warmth and strength of his wonderful body against hers.

"Oh, Dake," she murmured, but the words were muffled as their mouths clung urgently together, seeking reassurance from one another, seeking each other's hidden sweetness.

Dake's hands moved down her back, pulling her even closer, and Melissa pressed herself against him. She could feel the taut muscles of his thighs shifting as he balanced himself on the rough flooring beneath the stadium stands, and she supported him with her own strength, wrapping her arms around him. His leather jacket was rough and cool; Melissa could feel it against her forearms where the sleeves of her sweater had been pushed up a little. A sweet fragrance filled the space between them as Dake's body crushed the petals of the carnation.

Melissa held him close for a moment longer, then pushed away, gasping for breath.

"Dake, I can't," she whispered quickly. "I have to go to the game."

He stepped back, too. When he spoke, his voice was hoarse and low. "Stay with me, Melissa." Then he smiled slowly, and his voice was stronger. "After all, I'm the biggest game around."

Melissa shook her head frantically. "I can't, Dake. I . . . I want to, but . . ."

They had both shoved their hands into their pockets, and they stood about a foot apart, watching each other.

"Mel, I'm serious. I need you to trust, to teach me how to trust. I feel as if I've had blinders on all these years."

Melissa shook her head, more slowly now. "Listen to

yourself," she said. "One minute you're the game and I'm the hunter, and the next minute you're asking me for some kind of emotional . . . I can't keep up, Dake."

She hesitated, aware that Dake's eyes were no longer on her face. He was watching someone above her, on the stairs.

"Quarry!" boomed President Warren's voice. "And Melissa!"

Melissa swung her head around abruptly. President Warren was standing halfway down the stairs, grinning. "Just grabbing a hot dog before the kickoff. I didn't get a damn thing to eat at the party. Too busy talking." He moved on down the stairs and headed toward the food concession. "Game starts in a couple of minutes," he called back over his shoulder. "See you there!"

Melissa closed her eyes. "Terrific," she muttered, "just terrific. Now Jack Warren thinks I'm—"

"What?" Dake interrupted. "Doing your job? Don't tell me it's bad for your reputation to be seen with me," he added lightly.

Melissa shook her head. "It's so confusing, Dake; there're just too many roles to play here. You have to realize that."

He looked at her steadily. "Okay. Maybe. But I can tell you one thing: I'm sure as hell not going to any football game. Meet me afterward."

Melissa studied his face. He looked confident and amused now; there was hardly a trace of the confused vulnerability she had heard in his voice just moments before, in his plea that she help him. But that didn't change things: She wanted him more than anything else in the world.

Impulsively, she reached into her shoulder bag and pulled out the key to her apartment. "Here," she said. "It's 106 Elm. I'll meet you there after the game."

- 5 -

THE DOOR OF the old house was unlocked when Melissa got back after the game late in the afternoon. She pushed it open and climbed the stairs to her rooms slowly, one hand on the polished wooden railing. All was silent behind the carved French doors leading to the doctor's office that occupied the ground floor. Upstairs was quiet as well.

Maybe he just left the door open for me, Melissa told herself nervously. And left the key on the table and went home. She smiled wryly. Maybe there'll be a bottle there, too, marked DRINK ME. Maybe he's disappeared again, just like the Cheshire Cat.

But Dake's leather flight jacket was hung on a hook at the top of the stairs under Melissa's small collection of hats, and his white running shoes, socks tucked neatly inside, were sitting by the door of the living room. He seemed to have a thing about not wearing shoes, she noted in amusement.

Dake himself was stretched out on the long couch, his bare feet propped up on its arm and a pillow under

73

his head. He was holding a brochure that Melissa had been working on for class reunions the following spring, studying it critically.

He turned his head as she entered the room.

"Welcome home," he said brightly.

Melissa glanced around. Nothing seemed disturbed; nothing was out of place. She had expected him to be somehow too big for her warren of rooms, to throw the whole apartment out of kilter, but he looked precisely at home right where he was. He seemed to belong there, in among the dried flowers and the black-and-white photos in their ancient frames and the thrift-shop furniture Melissa had lovingly stripped and refinished to a soft glow.

"Hi," she answered breezily. She busied herself with her things, fussily unwrapping the scarf from her neck, setting the floppy shoulder bag down carefully by the big chair. Then she began working at the carnation pin, trying to undo it, but her hands just wouldn't function properly.

Dake balanced the brochure on his stomach.

"Come over here," he said, "and I'll get that for you."

Melissa glanced at him. "It's okay," she muttered. She moved to the mirror, smoky with age, hanging on one wall and pulled at the pin again. It caught on her heavy sweater, snagging it. "Damn."

Dake shifted on the couch, and the brochure fell to the floor. He reached down and smoothed it with one hand, checking to make sure it hadn't creased, then propped himself up on his elbow. "Come over here, Mel."

Melissa stared at her image a moment longer in the mirror. Her cheeks were bright pink from the hours of outdoor cold at the stadium, and her hair looked blowsy; great springy curls had pulled out from the ribbon she had gathered them into, and the wind had left them a chaos of tangles. She patted at it ineffectually.

"Mel," Dake said softly again, drawing out the single syllable into a cajoling melody. He tossed a small pillow across the room at her.

Melissa turned, took the several steps to his side, and knelt in front of where he lay on the couch. With long, graceful fingers, Dake unpinned the carnation easily and laid it on the table beside a glass bowl full of colored marbles. He tapped the little snag back into place.

"Will you keep it?" he asked with a wave at the flower.

Melissa looked at him quizzically. "Whatever for?" she said uncertainly. He had turned on a single lamp in the room, at the head of the couch, and it made a small pool of light around his face. His eyes sparkled darkly as he looked at her.

He waved a hand around the room, encompassing the various knickknacks and souvenirs and objets d'art Melissa had collected over the years. "You seem to be a saver."

She smiled, then shrugged. "Maybe I will," she said.

She was still kneeling by the couch, and Dake lifted one hand to her face and lightly traced a line down her cheek, from temple to chin. His finger trailed easily along her soft skin, and wherever it touched, Melissa's flesh responded with a shivery warmth that seemed to echo endlessly, reverberating in ever-larger circles, until it invaded the most hidden spaces of her body. She looked down, seeking relief from his eyes, and her gaze caught the brochure.

She rocked back on her heels, the flyer in her hand. "Thinking about coming to a reunion?" she asked, self-consciously casual. "It'll be your fifteenth."

Dake rolled onto his back and looked at the ceiling. He picked up another small pillow and began tossing it into the air. "Am I allowed? As a non-graduate?"

Abruptly Melissa remembered her shock at the news he had delivered earlier, that he had never graduated. Her brow furrowed in a frown. "Is that really true?" she asked.

Dake glanced at her, and the pillow fell behind the couch. "Of course it's true. You must know that. You're such a pro at your job, you've certainly read my transcript by now."

Melissa shook her head slowly, and the frown turned into a little smile that tugged at the corners of her mouth.

"No. It's embarrassing, to tell you the truth. I sort of stuck it away after I got it—your student file—and I just never got back to it." She glanced up at him mischievously. "But I read all those newspaper articles about you."

Dake looked skeptical. "Ah. The *Daily Collegian*, fountainhead of truth and justice. But how're you ever going to catch me in your money-grubbing nets if you don't have *all* the information?"

He smiled sweetly, but Melissa felt a very real twinge of annoyance.

She stood up. "Dake, I thought we'd settled this. I'm not trying to catch you. Or rather, I am, but I'm trying very hard to keep my professional interest in you separate from . . ."

"From?" Dake repeated. He pushed himself up on both hands, swung his feet off the arm of the couch, and looked at her steadily with wide, inquisitive eyes. His smile was, if anything, even more innocent. "From what?" he asked again.

Melissa moved back across the room, away from the touch of his hand, away from the sweetness of his smile. She sat down in the overstuffed chair across from the couch and pulled her boots off, then tucked her feet underneath her. The heavy Irish sweater was beginning to feel very warm.

"Why didn't you graduate?" she asked.

Dake sat up all the way and faced her, crossing an ankle over one knee. He began absently massaging his calf with slow, almost mechanical motions, as though this was something he had done so many times before that he did it now without thinking.

"I *wanted* to graduate," he said slowly. He was staring at the wall behind Melissa, and he seemed hardly aware of her presence as he spoke. "I wanted a Ransom degree. I wanted to prove—" Abruptly his sober mood broke, and he looked at Melissa and laughed. "But it was not to be," he said lightly. "Too bad. My parents never went to college, so it was really important to them."

He continued to rub his leg; then, as if he had suddenly become aware of what he was doing, he stopped and tucked his hands into the pockets of his jeans. He was wearing another turtleneck, this one camel-colored and a little heavier than the blue one he had worn on Friday. The sweater made soft, comfortable curves of the hard angles of his body.

"Well, what happened?" Melissa said impatiently. "There must have been some other money around somewhere. You didn't need to quit just because they took your scholarship away."

Dake looked at her steadily for a moment, as if she were something of vague scientific interest. Then he sighed and moved his gaze back to the wall.

"I didn't just quit," he said. "At first, when they took my money away, I thought I'd do about anything to stay at Ransom. I found a night job on the line at this little shoe factory near Elgin. It paid good money. But I needed a car to get to it, so my parents pulled together what they could and bought me one. Problem was, the whole thing ate away at my study time. My grades started down."

He pulled one hand out of his pocket and automatically began massaging his leg again.

"My parents got nervous about the grades. They went into debt—way beyond a farmer's normal debt—so I could cut back on the time I worked. For spring semester, I went to part-time, and things were a little better. I figured it was doable." The movement of his hand was almost hypnotic, going round and round in circles on his calf. Melissa watched and listened intently.

"In the summer I pushed back up to full-time at the plant and found a room out there so I wouldn't have to commute."

Melissa leaned forward in her chair, her brow creased in concern. "Didn't you tell Ransom what was going on?" she asked. "Wouldn't they have helped? Wasn't there *anybody* you trusted?"

Dake blinked and looked at her, again as if he were noticing her for the first time. He shook his head and shrugged.

"A professor or two," he said. He rubbed his chin lightly, seeming to consider her words. "And yeah, maybe they would have helped. But I sure didn't think so at the time. We'd made a deal, and the deal was no longer valid. Ransom had taken back its money." He shrugged again. "That was that."

He let his long, lithe body relax, sinking back against the couch. Melissa felt a growing need to touch him, to go and sit beside him and feel his strength beside her—and to lend him a little of her own. She shifted in her chair.

"So anyway, then the car broke down," he went on. "And it was a bad year for sugar beets. There wasn't a farthing left in the pot. And that, as the saying goes, was that."

Melissa shook her head fiercely. "So *then* you quit? Without even giving Ransom a chance to help?"

Dake raised his eyebrows. "I was supposed to crawl back and offer—what? I'd told Rudge I'd be ready to run again the fall of my senior year, and he'd made it clear he wasn't interested. I was out of bargaining chips."

"You don't have to bargain for scholarships, Dake. There's money available for talented students. There always has been. Without your giving anything in return except your willingness to learn."

Dake smiled. It was a small, tight smile, without a hint of amusement in it. "That didn't seem to be the way the game was played at Ransom. Nobody told me there were any other rules," he said quietly. "And nobody paid much attention when I didn't turn up in the fall."

"How could..." Melissa paused and looked down at the floor. The hell with it, she decided. Let him know how you feel. She looked up again, straight into Dake's dark eyes. "How could nobody pay attention?" she asked. "How could they possibly not notice? You're one of the most noticeable people I've ever met."

Dake's eyes stayed steady on her own, and slowly, very slowly, a smile turned up the corners of his mouth. He rose from the couch, stepped around the coffee table, then let himself down gently onto his knees on the rug in front of her chair. He put both hands on the arms of the chair, catching her in the circle of his own arms without touching her. Then he buried his face in her lap.

Melissa touched his head, touched the softness of his thick, dark hair once again, and stroked it gently. "Oh, Dake," she whispered.

"I need you, Mel," he murmured.

They stayed that way for several moments; the only movement in the room was the slow, gentle stroke of Melissa's hand through his hair. Then he lifted his face and looked at her.

If he had reached for her in the way she expected him to, pulling her face down to his for a kiss, she knew she might have said no. But instead he took his hands from the arms of the chair and lifted her heavy woolen sweater and the cotton turtleneck as well. Slowly, he leaned forward and kissed the naked ivory flesh just above her waist.

Melissa felt a harsh shudder race through her, unlike the small, pleasant shivers she had felt on other occasions from Dake's presence or his touch. This time it was a trembling that shook her whole body; it was exquisitely painful, and it made her gasp out loud. Her breathing quickened as Dake's mouth trailed over the vulnerable flesh, leaving warmth behind wherever it touched. He pushed the sweater higher.

"Dake, please . . ." she began, but he looked up at her and smiled.

"Shh," he said softly.

Something at the very center of Melissa collapsed, some pocket of resistance. Suddenly there was a turbulence there, inside her, like a great windstorm; everything seemed to be tumbling over itself, splintering, shattering like fine glass into the tiniest fragments. She nodded, entranced by Dake's dark eyes.

He grasped the bottom of her two sweaters with both hands, and in one graceful motion he pulled them up and over her head, then laid them on the floor beside the chair.

He drew in a sharp breath. Her full breasts strained against the satiny wisp of cloth that enclosed them. Dake closed his eyes for a mere moment, then reached behind her, slid the straps down over her arms, and let the thin fabric fall to the floor. Melissa felt a sudden, unbidden sense of freedom, and she instinctively stretched both arms above her head, her breasts taut and firm.

Dake rocked back on his heels and watched her with half-closed eyes. "Oh, Lord," he said finally, his voice hoarse. Melissa smiled at him and lowered her arms again.

He touched a finger to one breast, gently, tentatively, and Melissa felt the shiver begin there and race through her body again until she was trembling all over. Dake pulled back for a moment, then laid his whole hand against the side of her breast.

She buried both hands in his hair. His breathing was quick and shallow as he pressed his mouth against the silken flesh before him, and Melissa felt a series of tiny, exquisite explosions as his mouth and tongue explored her breasts, finding the hollow between them and their dark, erect tips. For a moment longer, his mouth teased her, and the trembling in her body continued.

Then Dake raised his face to hers, and the teasing ended abruptly. Their lips met at last, and Melissa opened herself to him, her mouth wide in urgent desiring, her teeth nipping at his lips, her tongue meeting his. Eagerly, impatiently, she pulled at his sweater until he held his arms high and allowed her to slide it off over his head. She let it fall beside them, her mouth seeking his again with a need so strong that her whole body ached with it.

He still knelt on the floor in front of her. Melissa wrapped her legs around him, imprisoning him within the circle of herself, but Dake pushed himself up inside the circle and lifted her as well. His strong arms pulled her from the chair, holding her body hard against his own, and then lowered her gently onto the thick rug that covered the floor. They faced each other, kneeling, and Melissa twisted against him, her hands at his back. His chest felt cool, soothing, against the throbbing heat of her breasts. Melissa let a small sigh escape as her mouth traced a path of kisses along his cheek.

Dake undid the waistband of her slacks and slid them down below her hips. She could hear his agonized breathing as she shifted her weight, letting him push the slacks off altogether. He buried his face in her hair, his mouth against her ear. He felt smooth and sleek beneath her hands, like a cat, his muscles long and graceful and lithe. Melissa felt catlike herself, as though they were moving together through the high savannah grass, slowly at first, then faster, gathering speed together, side by side, the sharp grass sliding off the sleek lines of their bodies as they ran . . .

Melissa fumbled with the snap of Dake's jeans, and he laid a hand on hers, trying to help. They were both clumsy; fingers that had been strong and able only moments before now were made useless by urgency. Finally the snap gave, and she pushed his jeans aside. She could feel the hardness of him against her belly.

Dake pulled her down next to him on the thick rug, and their shaking hands explored each other's bodies. Melissa said his name softly and pressed him to her, her hands against the flat of his back. Soon their bodies began to move together in a single rhythm, shifting this way and that in exquisite harmony, seeking satisfaction—as if they had always known each other, great wildcats raised together on the vast plains.

At last Dake rolled onto her and came to her, and the silken, muscular cats leaped in unison across some unthinkable chasm and landed together on the other side, panting, exhausted, agonizingly fulfilled. Melissa heard herself cry out his name.

Eventually, her heavy breathing began to slow, and Melissa shifted away from Dake's long body and flung her arms out to her sides. She concentrated on getting her breathing back under control.

After a moment, she glanced over at Dake. He was propped on one elbow, looking at her. His body was damp with perspiration, and the bronze skin seemed to glow in the soft light of the single lamp.

"You're beautiful," he said quietly.

Melissa's gaze meandered slowly over his body, following the angular lines of his shoulders, the flat plane of his belly, the thick muscles of his thighs. Then her eyes settled back on his face, with its high cheekbones, its deep, dark eyes; its broad, sensual mouth. "You too," she said softly.

Dake laughed.

The harsh urgency of their coming together had faded, and Melissa pushed herself up on her hands, then stood.

Dake watched her, lying back naked against the rug, his arms folded behind his head. There was a satisfied, almost smug smile on his face.

"Hungry?" he asked.

Melissa shook her head. Suddenly she felt shy, standing there in the middle of her living room with Dake's lanky frame stretched out across her rug. She folded her arms across her breasts.

"I need some clothes," she said.

He rolled over onto his stomach, as if he recognized her discomfort with his nakedness. "So soon?"

Melissa shrugged, then scooped up her clothing from the floor and scurried out of the room. In the bathroom, she splashed cold water from her old marble pedestal sink onto her face. The full import of what she had done began taking root.

Just what is it that you think you're doing? she asked herself sharply. Making love with this guy breaks every professional rule you know. What the *hell* do you think you're doing?

She caught her own gaze in the mirror and sighed. Having a glorious time, she answered. The best time of my whole life.

She pulled a terry-cloth robe off a bathroom hook and wrapped it tightly around herself, then hurried through the hall and into her bedroom. By the time she came back into the living room, dressed in jeans and a loose shirt, Dake was up and partly dressed himself, his jeans on but his chest still bare. He was carefully straightening the rug where they had tumbled together.

Melissa settled back into her chair.

He looked at her and grinned. "Sure you're not hungry?"

She shook her head again. "I feel full." She was uncomfortably conscious of his gleaming bronze chest. She glanced around the room, looking anywhere but at Dake, and realized with a start that all the curtains were still open. Quickly she padded around the room and drew them closed. Dake watched her, a puzzled look on his face.

"It's . . . I always feel I'm on display here after dark if the curtains are open," she explained weakly. "I'm only half a block off the main street."

Dake nodded. Melissa stood by the last window, the edge of the curtain still in her hand. "And maybe you could put your sweater back on," she added, her voice a little sharper than she might have wished.

He laughed. "Too much for you?" he asked. "I kind of like myself this way, actually." But he reached for his sweater where it lay on the floor and pulled it on over his head. "Better?" he asked while the sweater still covered his face, muffling his voice a little.

Melissa nodded as his head appeared through the turtleneck. "Better," she agreed.

He sat back down on the couch and crossed a bare foot over one knee. Better still if he'd put his damn socks on, she told herself. But that would sound absolutely perverse.

She sat down on the couch beside him. Her body felt tender from their lovemaking, and she shifted gingerly against the pillows, then picked up a small one and turned it slowly in her hands, wondering where to go from here.

"Tell me about your doctor husband," Dake said after a moment's silence, turning toward her. "I feel as if I don't know anything about you."

Melissa smiled wryly. "*You* don't know anything about me? You just found out things about me that *I* didn't even know."

Dake leaned his head against the back of the couch and grinned. "Not that kind of thing," he said. "I mean little things. Facts. The kind of stuff you've been so successful in worming out of me."

Melissa tossed the pillow at him. "Alexander Markham the Third," she answered. "Sandy. He was . . ." She paused a moment, thinking, then went on. "He was thin and blond and intense and terribly committed to saving the world when we were in college. And very, very much in need of being taken care of."

Dake nodded. "I know the type. And you took care of him right through med school."

Melissa felt herself bristle. No matter what Sandy had or had not turned out to be, she had loved him once. And once, she knew, he had been deserving of that love.

"No," she said firmly. "It wasn't like that. He had no problems paying his way through med school. Besides, I was still here at Ransom most of the time."

She waited a moment for Dake to apologize, but he didn't. She shrugged. "But . . ." She paused and then sighed. "Now he's got a nice little paunch and a nice little bald spot, and he's terribly committed to making lots of money for himself. He's chief of surgery at a big hospital in Kansas City."

"So he got too ugly for you?"

She glanced at him sharply, but Dake was looking at her with an innocent grin.

Melissa made a face at him. "No. Maybe he got too
. . . safe. And maybe I got too liberated for him, among
other things. I decided to make a career out of my volunteer activities, and for some reason that frightened him.
I got my M.B.A., and that made him mad. Then when
he announced one night that we were moving from Chicago to Kansas City, that made *me* mad. And I told him
maybe he was moving, but I wasn't."

It sounded so simple, so painless in the retelling. But
even now, Melissa could feel the tears beginning way
down deep below the surface. She blinked her eyes to
keep them there.

Dake smiled. "Brave woman," he said softly. "You
really loved him."

Melissa looked at him gratefully.

"Yes," she said.

"I guess," he said slowly, "it's hard for me to understand that. I got married once, but it was basically the
same kind of deal I'd signed with Ransom."

Melissa's eyes widened. "How can you call a marriage
a deal?"

Dake smiled and shrugged. "That tends to be the way
I look at things. Like I told you this afternoon."

"It sounds so . . . callous," she said hesitantly. She
picked up another pillow and held it against her stomach,
wanting to have something to hold on to.

Dake looked at her with half-closed eyes. "I guess I
learned my lessons well here at Ransom," he said.

Melissa rolled her eyes. "You can't go through life
blaming everything on one event, Dake. On evil old
Ransom College. At some point you've got to take some
responsibility yourself."

Dake leaned forward and rested his elbows on his
knees, his chin in his hands. "I thought I'd gotten over
it, Mel. I honestly did. This last year especially, I've
been thinking about all of it now and then. Some of the
things *you've* been saying, too. How Ransom introduced
me to Chicago and gave me at least part of a fine education and—" He stopped abruptly and shook his head.

"But seeing Rudge at that dinner last week—I just hadn't realized how strongly I still felt. I don't know, Mel."

Melissa nodded. She remembered what he'd said earlier in the day, about needing her help. He had seemed so vulnerable. "Well, maybe we can work some of it out."

Dake's smile was thoughtful. "I'm not sure, Mel. I'm just not sure." He pulled the pillow away from her, then tossed it back playfully. "The party this afternoon was fine. I even liked Jack Warren. But what I'd really like for us, for you and me..." He hesitated and tapped her knee for emphasis. "What I want for us is to keep out of Ransom altogether. Just find a common ground, where Ransom doesn't play a role. Like..." His smile turned mischievous, and he waved a hand toward the rug in front of the fireplace. "Like there, for instance."

Melissa got to her feet. She still held the pillow pressed against her belly. "We can't just forget what I do, Dake. It's part of who I am. It's why we met."

He nodded. "But we can damn well do our best. We can, for instance, find ourselves some dinner."

"Dake..."

"And then..." He waggled his eyebrows in a mock leer.

Melissa turned away. The confusion she had been holding away by sheer force of will suddenly flooded through her again. It wasn't so much who *he* was that confused her; it was who *she* was. She turned back to face him.

"Dake, you have a long drive home."

His broad smile faded slowly. "I wasn't really anticipating making that drive tonight," he said softly.

Melissa put one hand on the arm of the chair for support. This was going to be a hard one, she knew.

"You can't stay here," she said.

He looked sincerely perplexed. "Why not?"

Melissa took in a deep breath and blew it out slowly. "You can't stay here, because, among other things, it wouldn't look right."

Dake rose, too, and there was a look of annoyed impatience on his handsome features.

"What the hell does *that* mean?"

Melissa shrugged. "What if someone saw you coming out of here in the morning? Half those people out there know me, and they know my job is to talk people out of their money. And at least some of them know that you're one of the people I'm supposed to talk money out of. So how's that going to look?"

"Like you happen to be sleeping with somebody you're also trying to talk money out of." Dake stood by the couch, his face out of the lamp's small pool of light. Melissa could see only his eyes and the outlines of his high cheekbones in the darkness. "So what? Give me some serious objections, Mel."

"I *am* serious, Dake!" she cried in frustration. "Some of the people I work with happen to think that's just the way I should be going about my job in the first place. I can't believe you agree with them!"

Dake stepped back into the light, as if he were suddenly aware that his face was a mystery to her.

"I just don't see why you give a damn what anybody else thinks," he said quietly. "I'd like to spend the night with you."

Melissa felt herself crumple slightly, and she leaned one hip against the chair.

"I know," she whispered. "But you can't. It's not just what people might say. It's me. Dake, I've been wheedling money out of people all my life. I've never felt this kind of confusion before. I can't figure out how to think about myself. I wish you'd understand."

Dake stood a moment longer, his eyes studying her face. Then he smiled a small smile. "I'll try," he said.

He moved across the room in three long, easy strides and came to a stop beside her. Quickly, he leaned down and brushed a kiss against her cheek. He stopped to pick up his shoes and socks from the floor by the living room door and to pull them on, and Melissa heard him take his flight jacket from the hook in the hall. His footsteps echoed on the uncarpeted staircase, and she heard the outside door close softly behind him.

Then she let the tears that had been waiting all that time well slowly from her eyes.

- 6 -

WHEN HE HAD GONE, Melissa put an early Rolling Stones album on the stereo, turned it up loud, and spent the next hour compulsively removing every trace of Dake Quarry from her apartment. She plumped up the pillows on the couch, put the brochure layout back on the table, and straightened the rug yet again. But she knew it wouldn't work. There was no denying that he had invaded her private space in every sense.

She shook her head wryly at the thought. You could hardly call it an invasion, she told herself. More like a response to an open invitation. And she had only herself to blame.

She called Luigi's and ordered a pizza with everything, to be delivered as soon as possible.

On Monday morning, still in her jogging suit, Melissa headed for the field house, where the athletic department offices were housed.

"Susie," she panted, breathless from her run to campus, "Mr. Rudge in?"

The pretty dark-haired girl nodded. "Want to see him, Miss Markham?"

"Yes. If he has time."

Susie picked up the intercom phone, and a moment later the door swung open behind her and Robert Rudge appeared.

"Well, mornin', ma'am. It's a treat to see your pretty face this early. Come on in." He gestured Melissa into his thickly carpeted office. She passed the floor-to-ceiling trophy case with hardly a glance.

"What can I do for you this morning, darlin'? You want some coffee?" he asked, lowering his bulk into the big swivel chair behind his desk. "Susie!" he bellowed before she could answer. "Coffee!"

Melissa started to shake her head, but Susie was already in the room, coffee pot in hand. She poured out a cup for Melissa and refilled Rudge's red and white mug. He raised it toward Melissa.

"Cheers."

Melissa took a sip and waited until Rudge had swallowed a gulp of his.

"Bob," she said finally, "I was wondering about a few things. It's really none of my business, but—"

Rudge made an expansive gesture with one arm, as though taking in the whole field house. "We're all family, missy. You got to have the facts to raise your money. Anything you want to know, you just ask."

"Well..." Now that she was here, Melissa wasn't exactly sure what it was she did want. "I was really just curious about a couple of things that have . . . come up. I wondered if athletes still live up at Harper, the way they used to when I was in school. And whether or not they're required to take specific schedules."

Rudge leaned forward over his desk and folded his meaty hands in front of him. The expression on his face was earnest and sympathetic, like a teacher about to try to instill some basic concepts in a particularly dense student.

"Now, who you been talking to, darlin'? Don't you know you can't tell anybody *anything* anymore—not where to live, not what courses to take. Nothin'. And that's no matter if they're taking money from us or not. Wouldn't stand for it, these kids today. It used to help, having 'em all in one place like that, for training table and all. Now . . ." He shook his head a little sadly. "We've got no control anymore. No control."

He picked up a pencil and made a single check mark on a big yellow pad that lay on his desk blotter.

"So, no, the athletes don't live in Harper anymore. Now as to courses, well, we give advice, just like we've always done. Sometimes we think a boy—or a *girl*," he interjected with a quick smile. "We got scholarship athlete *girls* now, darlin'. So sometimes it seems to us that this boy or girl would get a little more out of school if they followed some particular plan of study. That's all. Just a little advice."

He nodded, and his chins sank into one another like downy pillows. "A little advice. Nothing wrong with that."

Melissa looked at him speculatively. "You mean there are certain professors who cater to athletes?"

"Nope," Rudge answered immediately. "Nobody caters. Anybody gets into Ransom deserves to be here, missy. Our athletic admissions board understands that. But some courses, well, they provide a little *more* for our boys and girls."

Melissa nodded slowly. "Is that who awards scholarships? Your admissions board?"

"We have an alumni board, darlin'. We work with the regular admissions people. But we make recommendations."

She nodded again. "What about injuries?" she asked.

Rudge leaned back in his chair. "I don't follow, missy."

"When someone gets hurt. Someone on scholarship. Do they lose the scholarship?"

Rudge's eyes narrowed. "Now who you been talkin' to?" he asked. "There're rules about that kind of—" Suddenly the folds of his eyelids rose so that his bright blue eyes were entirely visible for the first time. "You been talkin' to Mr. Dake Quarry! Haven't you now, darlin'? You been talkin' to Mr. Quarry. Yessir."

He settled back again with an expression of complete satisfaction on his face.

Melissa took a deep breath. "Yes, as a matter of fact," she said, "I have. Mr. Quarry had a few complaints about the way scholarships were administered when he was here, and I thought, since he has a good deal of money to give, that I'd better check out—"

"I bet he did!" Rudge interrupted with a chuckle that was more like a wheeze. "I just bet he did. Well, Ransom College had a few complaints about Mr. Dake Quarry, too, darlin'. You can just bet we did."

"Like what?"

Melissa sat still in her chair, her hands folded in her lap. She suddenly wished she had gone to her own office first and changed; sitting here in her yellow jogging suit, she felt a little like one of Rudge's athletes, called in for a conference.

"Well, Mr. Quarry was a hell-raiser, missy, not to mention a complainer. Downright whiny, he was. Now I guess you could understand it; here we swooped in and took him out of his teeny tiny town up there in Colorado and gave him some national recognition. Out of his depth, I suspect."

Melissa's hands tightened in her lap. "I thought he was a national junior champion before he came here."

Rudge dismissed her remark with a wave. "High school isn't quite the same thing, darlin'. He'd had a little taste of being the best, and it went to his head. Then he got here, and found out he'd have to *work* at it, and . . ."

He shrugged, his massive shoulders rising eloquently toward his ears. "Mr. Quarry wanted things his own way. Now he kept to training, I'll give him that. But he was a troublemaker. Played pranks. Complained. Chased the women some. Had a good eye for the women, I must say." He winked conspiratorially. A knot that felt as big as a fist formed in Melissa's stomach.

"Now we could forgive him his wild oats," Rudge went on, "because the boy sure could run. Thing we couldn't really forgive was that Mr. Quarry just didn't want to be coached. Didn't understand how the system worked. Nossir. And then he got hurt." He drummed the fingers of one hand on his desk for a moment. "Junior year, I think."

"He tore an Achilles tendon," Melissa said flatly.

Rudge nodded. "That was it. And he got temperamental about it. Real temperamental."

"He tore it a second time," she pushed on, "because he was forced to run too soon after the injury. And when he wouldn't compete anymore, you took his scholarship away."

Rudge rose partway out of his chair, then sat back again. He shook his head slowly, his eyes wide with innocence. "Nobody forced anybody, darlin'. Mr. Quarry refused to carry out his part of the scholarship contract, despite the opinion of our team physician. He let us down, pure and simple. It was a fair decision."

A smile trailed slowly across his face. He picked up the pencil again and made a second check mark.

"Besides," he added, "looking at him now, I don't see that it did a whole lot of hurt."

Melissa felt the knot in her stomach expand a little. She knew she was angry, but she sensed, too, that some of the knot was doubt.

"He had to leave school," she said a little less sharply. "He never even graduated. Because he didn't have the money to finish."

Rudge looked at her for a moment, his eyes wide and blue again. Then he exploded into laughter. He sucked in breath between laughs, and after a moment he wiped his eyes to clear the tears.

"Is that what he told you, darlin'?" he asked finally. "That he left and went home broke with his tail between his legs because Ransom took his money away?"

Melissa nodded, but the doubts were beginning to outweigh the anger. A frown furrowed her brow.

"Well, let me show you somethin'," Rudge said.

He pushed himself up from the chair, both hands on his desk, and his body almost seemed to inflate as he rose. He moved slowly over to an old gray metal filing cabinet at one side of the office. He pulled a drawer out, then had to stand for a moment and catch his breath from the effort.

"Here," he said finally, holding out a battered manila folder. "Let me show you somethin' here."

He made his slow progress back, lowered himself again into the chair, and pushed the folder across the desk toward Melissa. She leaned forward to open it. Inside was an article clipped from *Time* magazine some fifteen years earlier. The headline was *Sports: How to Make an Easy Million*. She glanced at it quickly—something about Americans playing basketball in Italy.

"I don't understand," she said, looking up at Rudge.

He waved a hand toward the faded pages. "Read it, darlin'."

Melissa skimmed the article. Its point seemed to be that fortune and fame were to be had in Italian professional basketball for those who couldn't quite make it in the N.B.A. She shook her head.

"I still don't—"

"Right down there in the last paragraph," Rudge interrupted a little impatiently.

Melissa looked down again. Listed among the Americans who had come to Italy to make their millions was Dakin Quarry. She read the paragraph through twice.

"Now." Rudge put both fat hands on his desk, palms down. "Mr. Quarry told you he left here because he was broke. But two months later he was playin' pro ball in Italy and livin' like a king. Are you gonna tell me he didn't have that offer in his hand when he quit college?"

The slow smile spread across his face again, like peanut butter spread with a knife.

"Are you gonna tell me he didn't leave here because somebody came along with a better deal?"

Melissa folded the article slowly and placed it back in the open manila folder. She brushed an imaginary piece of lint off her jogging pants, then stood up.

"Thanks very much, Bob," she said, holding out a hand to shake. "You've been very helpful."

Rudge rose with an effort and took her hand between both of his. "Yes, ma'am," he said, "you just come visit anytime at all. But you watch what you believe, now." He winked again. "Did you find out what you wanted to know?"

"I'm not sure," she said hesitantly.

"Well," he added, "you just come back when you need more. Old Coach is always here."

Melissa could still hear his wheezing as she disappeared out the door of his office.

Back in her own office, she hurried past Jeff with a quick "Good morning" and collapsed into her chair. She rested her head in her hands. No matter how complex the conflict between job and emotions, she had never really doubted Dake's truthfulness. She had assumed he was a good man, even if his bitterness toward Ransom seemed sometimes to outweigh his good sense. But if he had lied to her about his reasons for leaving Ransom . . .

He had accused her of laying a trap for him. Was it possible that he was doing just that to her? Setting her up for some kind of . . . She shook her head. *Revenge* was an ugly word.

There was a timid knock on the door, and Melissa looked up to find Jeff entering the office.

"Am I allowed in?" he asked.

She took a deep breath and nodded.

"You look bad," Jeff said thoughtfully. "Tough weekend? And you're late. A first for Ms. Markham."

Melissa grimaced at him. "Thanks for all the support and reassurance, Jeffrey. I appreciate it."

He smiled sleepily. "Hey, it's Monday morning. It's

the best I can do. But really, you okay? You do look a little dragged out." He sounded genuinely concerned, and Melissa sat up straight and smiled at him.

"I just came from Bob Rudge's office," she said. "I need a minute to recover."

"Ah." Jeff nodded wisely. "That'll do it. Tell you what. Disappear into the bathroom, wash your face, change your clothes, and you'll feel like a new woman. We got Christmas cards to deal with."

Melissa stood up. "Right. The all-purpose solution for the new woman," she muttered. "Bury yourself in your work. Sort of like buying a hat used to be."

Jeff chuckled. "Why were you seeing the coach?" he asked as Melissa scooped up her backpack and headed for the bathroom door.

"Oh..." She stopped and planted a hand on her hip. Why *had* she gone to see Rudge? To find out how the athletics programs were run? Or to check up on Dake? "Just to get some idea of how he does things over there," she said firmly, making her decision. "And I didn't get much."

She pushed the door open.

Jeff's usually lazy eyes were wide with interest. "Wanna be starting something?" he asked.

"With the athletics department? Are you crazy?" Melissa shook her head. "Actually, I don't know. I've just been hearing some stuff..." She chewed for a second at one fingernail. "The other day he offered to use college funds to buy Windflame shoes. In return for a hefty contribution from Dake."

"Dake?" Jeff raised an eyebrow, then smiled. "Dake. Okay. Yeah, I heard a lot of stories about how Bobby Rudge spends his money when I was in school here."

Melissa stood with one hand on the bathroom door. "Such as?" she asked.

Jeff shrugged. "Want me to do some digging?"

"Jeffrey, you're incurable." She smiled. "Only if you've got time. We have a major gifts campaign to run, after all." She pushed on through the door and let it swing shut behind her.

Her secretary had been right. By the time she had washed and changed, Melissa *did* feel better. Dake Quarry was a problem that would have to be resolved—there was no denying that—but it was a problem she could bury under other problems for a few weeks. At least until after Christmas. If she could just keep him out of her dreams, she was certainly efficient enough to keep him out of her work.

And Lord knows I have enough work, she told herself with a glance at the piles of folders on her desk. A post-Christmas trip to be coordinated, continuing research on alumni that hadn't yet been tapped, et cetera. Lots to do.

It wasn't until Wednesday that the Christmas mailing was entirely under control. Melissa spent two hours at a luncheon meeting with Alan McAllister and several out-of-town alumni. When she returned to her desk, she found a message scrawled on a sheet of legal paper. *Call Dake,* it read.

"Jeffrey!" she yelled, picking up the note between thumb and forefinger, as though it might bite.

Jeff's head appeared around the edge of the door. "Yo."

"You take this message?"

He stepped into the office. "Yes, ma'am."

Melissa held out the sheet of yellow paper. "Did he call himself Dake?" she asked sternly. "Or was that the Jeffrey touch?"

"Oh, he called himself that. Just Dake. No Quarry or anything." Jeff nodded earnestly.

Melissa glared at her secretary for a moment, then sighed. "Okay. Thanks. Anything else?"

Jeff pulled a hand from behind his back and studied the list it held. "Call from Phil Donlon at the alumni office. He's going east after Christmas, and he wants to talk about who he should see about the campaign. Also one from Alan McAllister. Says he's going to Phoenix next week, and have we got anybody there he should talk to. Also one from that guy at the Ford Foundation."

Melissa settled back into her chair, swiveled to one side, and stretched her long legs straight out in front of her. She nodded slowly. "Have we got any alums in Phoenix worth pursuing?" she asked.

"Three," Jeff answered promptly. "Want me to handle that one? And I've mapped out a few contacts for Phil Donlon, too. So you can get right back to Dake Quarry. Here's his number." Jeff smiled innocently. "Want me to get him for you?"

Melissa stuck out her tongue. "You are *transparent,* Jeffrey. No. I'm busy. I'll get to it later."

But as soon as her secretary had left the office, Melissa dialed the Elgin number. This time she listened to The Band for several minutes before Dake got on the line.

"Hi, Mel. Listen, things are out of hand here. I can't talk. Can we do some shopping on Saturday? Watertower Place? I'll meet you by the escalator in the Michigan Avenue lobby. Twelve noon. Okay?"

Melissa hesitated for a moment. "Do I get to talk during this phone call?" she asked.

Dake laughed. "Sorry. I want to see you. Things to say. Downtown seemed like neutral territory."

"Well, I'd like to see you, too." Melissa's voice sounded a little grim to her own ears, but Dake didn't seem to notice.

"Terrific!" he cried. "Twelve o'clock."

"Dake . . ." She paused again, hearing Bob Rudge's accusations echo in her head.

"I really can't talk, love. Will I see you there? Yes?"

"Yes."

"Good."

Melissa heard the click at the other end of the line, then slowly lowered her own receiver into the cradle. Terrific, Markham, she told herself sharply. You need to have a major discussion with the guy, and he's planning on doing his Christmas shopping. That is *not* the environment you need.

But on the other hand, she thought as she punched the intercom button for Jeff to return and go over the afternoon's work, there's no chance I'll end up making love to him in the middle of Watertower Place. No chance at all. And *that's* a good thing. Talk about neutral territory!

She had consolidated the various information on Dake Quarry into one file folder—his undergraduate papers, copies of the campus newspaper articles, and everything else Jeff and two other assistants had gathered over the course of the last few weeks. Now she pulled the file to the center of her desk and skimmed through it one more time. There was no hint here of why he had left school. His transcript showed the slipping grades in his third year, and then the information simply stopped. No more course grades, no more items in the paper.

On top of the file was a note from President Warren, written to confirm his first phone call about Dake Quarry. *Full speed ahead,* it urged. Melissa studied it for a moment. "I really wanted a Ransom degree," she heard Dake saying. With a little sigh, she made a note across the bottom of the president's memo: *Never graduated,* she wrote. *Honorary degree as bait?*

She smiled a little wanly. Just doing her job, she told herself firmly.

Michigan Avenue on the first Saturday of December sparkled with excitement. Christmas lights and banners lined the length of the Million Dollar Mile, and the pinkish-white marble of Watertower Place gleamed in the bright winter sunlight. It had snowed just a little the day before, and patches of white were still visible here and there along the sidewalk. Melissa smiled as she skirted the old yellow stone water tower and, miraculously, found a parking place on the street.

It was two minutes before noon when she pushed through the revolving door into the main lobby and saw Dake coming through the door opposite. She caught her breath. The size of him was familiar to her now—his height, the width of his shoulders, the length of his muscular legs. But the wonders of his face always seemed new and agonizingly attractive.

Dake was half a head taller than anyone else in the crowded glass-enclosed lobby, and he cut through the milling throng with long, graceful strides, as though all those people simply didn't exist. His bronzed cheeks were glowing from the cold, and his hair lay full and neat against his handsome head. His eyes seemed to glitter with the same excitement that the Avenue itself had.

Melissa smiled and waved a gloved hand. It was clear that Dake could reach her faster than she could reach him, so she stopped and waited at the foot of the escalators leading to the next level of the mall. Behind her, the entrance to Lord & Taylor's revolved continuously; across the lobby, the door to Marshall Field's did the same.

Dake stopped in front of her and put a hand on her shoulder, as if he couldn't see her without touching her. Melissa felt the familiar little shiver of response. She smiled brightly.

"Hi," he said softly, leaning toward her so she could hear him over the din. "I've missed you."

Then he leaned closer still, and suddenly his mouth was covering her own in a kiss hardly made for public consumption. Melissa tried once, weakly, to push him away, but her body was betraying her; she wanted to feel the sweet urgency of his mouth against hers, the strength of his body against hers. She slid her hands around his waist, catching at the belt loops of his jeans, pulling him close. Even through the layers of leather and wool, she could feel his heat.

His tongue flickered into her mouth briefly, teasing, and then it was Dake who pulled away. He was grinning broadly.

"Hi again," he said as he took her elbow and turned her toward the UP escalator. "Let's go get lunch and plan the day."

Melissa nodded and stepped onto the moving staircase. Beside them, a waterfall tumbled elegantly along the length of the escalator, and glittering glass Christmas decorations hung from tiny trees. She could almost forget that Dake Quarry had lied to her—or at least bent the truth a little—about why he had left Ransom College.

She glanced across to the DOWN escalator, and she felt every nerve in her body tighten as her eyes caught the gaze of Bob Rudge. He was just opposite them, moving slowly down, his sausagelike fingers spread like a fan on the railing. He was smiling in a way Melissa could only characterize as a leer.

He waved, and she nodded in acknowledgment. Dake turned to follow the path of her gaze—just in time to see Rudge make a thumbs-up sign toward her and pass on by.

Something hard began to form in the pit of Melissa's stomach. Rudge had seen the kiss; she was sure of it. And God knew what he would do with that little piece of information. As they reached the top of the escalator and stepped off, she shook her head in silent frustration and tried to make herself smile again.

But Dake wasn't smiling. "What the hell was that all about?" he asked, his voice dangerously quiet. The crowds were sparser on the first mezzanine, and Melissa backed away a few steps, finding an out-of-the-way corner for them.

She shrugged and lied, "I have no idea. Just his way of saying hello, I guess." She looked at Dake, and her smile disappeared. His dark eyes were black with rage.

"He looked at you," Dake said, "and he gave you a signal. Like you were doing your job just right." He was watching Melissa with fiery eyes, his hands deep in the pockets of his flight jacket, as if he were afraid of their power.

Damn Bob Rudge, Melissa told herself fiercely. Damn him! "Dake, I told you that this might happen—I warned you the other night what some people might think if they saw us together." She didn't mention that Bob Rudge had started having his petty little thoughts even *before* he'd seen them together. Why add fuel to the fire?

Dake looked away for a moment, breathing heavily.

"Dake," she said cajolingly, "come on. Let's do some shopping."

But when he looked at her again, there was a small, tight smile on his lips.

"Maybe I'm not convinced he's thinking the wrong thing, Mel," he said quietly. "Maybe he's got it right after all."

Melissa's mouth fell open as anger flooded through her.

"Dammit, Dake," she said, "stop this. You're being damned insulting."

He nodded. "You certainly did a number on me. Before much longer I would have been handing the whole plant over to Ransom College. Maybe the rights to Windflame Runners, too."

Melissa stared at him. "So we're right back where we started," she said. "I thought we were trying to keep my job separate from . . . from the rest of this." She waved a hand in frustration.

Dake stared at her steadily as she spoke. "Maybe there *is* no rest of this," he said.

Melissa glared back. "If that's what you really believe, then why the hell do you think I'm here right now? Because Bob Rudge ordered me to be? Do you really think I'm in collusion with Rudge to bed you down? After what we've—"

Her voice was rising, and Melissa paused abruptly as two people turned from their own nearby conversation to look at her.

"Can't you accept anything as real emotion?" she asked, speaking more softly. "Don't you believe in anything at all?"

She could hear the quavery edge of impending tears in her voice, and she stopped.

Dake was still looking at her. He seemed to have

retreated somewhere behind his dark eyes; there was nothing showing there at all, no emotion.

"I actually believed in Alice in Wonderland for a minute there," he answered. "Now I'm beginning to believe that Wonderland's just like the rest of the world. Everybody's in on the deal."

Melissa felt the tension in her hands, clenched into gloved fists at her sides, and slowly relaxed them. "I'm sorry," she said finally. "I'm sorry that's the way you feel. But I've had my doubts about all this from the start, too, Dake. Someday I'd be interested in knowing just what *you've* been after these past few weeks. What kind of deal *you're* trying to make. But right now I'll be damned if I stand here and let you insult me."

She turned away abruptly and stepped onto the DOWN escalator, weaving her way through the crowd until she reached the bottom. As she stepped off, she glanced up once, quickly, but Dake's tall frame had disappeared.

- 7 -

SITTING IN THE middle of Melissa's desk on Monday morning was a thick, unfamiliar folder. She was in no mood for new projects, and she looked at it with distaste. The episode with Dake had left her exhausted and unhappy—although no doubt it was for the best, she told herself firmly. She would hand the whole Quarry business over to the president's office, or maybe to the alumni people. She would plead—she smiled—insanity, maybe.

She tucked one finger under the cover of the new folder and lifted it up. Some of the papers inside were covered with figures—copies, apparently, of account records. Others seemed to be letters—recruitment letters—and copies of notes about specific students. With a twinge of curiosity, she pulled it open.

The headings indicated that everything she was looking at had come from the athletic department.

"Jeff!" she called, punching the button on her desk as she realized what was in front of her.

Jeff ambled in.

She glared at him, waving a hand at the papers now spread over her desk. "What on earth *is* this stuff? And where on earth did you get it?"

He smiled a little smugly. "You said I could dig a little, if I had the time. So I had the time."

"When?" she exploded. "We've been going full-time on that Christmas mailing." She looked up at him, eyebrows raised.

Jeff shrugged. "My own time," he answered. "It's been an evening and weekend sort of project."

He stepped around the desk and sorted the papers quickly into piles. "Purchase records for the last few years for the athletic department, all requisitions signed personally by Robert Rudge, and inventory records. There are a few gaps between the two." He pointed to the second pile. "Recruitment records. Who promised what to whom." He moved his hand to the third pile. "And a few personal notes on which athletes put a roof on Bob's house for him. Stuff like that."

Melissa stared at the papers and shook her head slowly. "You're crazy, Jeff. You know that?" She tipped through one of the piles. "So what's here?" She looked up at him again.

"Enough to lose Rudge his job, if anybody with any sense of decency is in charge around here," he said happily.

"Are you implying that Rudge . . . just what *are* you implying?"

Jeff shrugged. "I wouldn't want to imply anything at all, boss. But there are a few requisitions for funds for equipment that just doesn't seem to exist. And then there's the assistant coach who promised an incoming lineman that he'd never have to worry about grades at Ransom. And what looks to me like a fudged transcript for last year's star linebacker. You just kind of read through these things, and they tend to speak for themselves."

Melissa kept her wide eyes on Jeff. "Okay. Let's start from the beginning. Where'd you get all this?"

His smile broadened. "Ways and means," he said. "You meet Susie over there, Mr. Rudge's secretary? Anyway," he added with another shrug, "it's all basically public information. He's a college employee."

"Doesn't he get audited every year?"

Jeff shook his head. "Our friend Mr. Coach pretty much has things his own way, it appears. No audits. Some deal he worked out with the president before Warren arrived on the scene."

Melissa rolled her eyes. "Jeff, I can't believe you. But we've got no business fooling around with all this. You should take it right on over to Warren's office."

"I don't think I'm the proper person," Jeff said with a shake of his red curls. "I think it should come from someone he knows and trusts. Like you."

Melissa sighed. "This does not make me happy."

Jeff frowned. "Boss, listen. This guy Rudge has run amok for years, apparently. He's wasted the college's money, and he's deprived the students he's recruited from taking full advantage of a Ransom education. Think of it that way. And now you have the chance to blow the whistle. Or at least to start some people thinking about what's been going on."

Melissa nodded slowly. "Of course you're right, Jeff. But I want to check it all myself before I pass it on to anyone." She looked down at the papers and studied them for a moment longer. "You're right, Jeff. If this stuff proves what you say, then it's important. I'll see if I can get an appointment with Warren before he leaves for the holidays."

"It is important," she said softly as she dialed the phone and listened to it ring.

"Hi, Donna," she said in her professional phone voice after a brief pause. "It's Melissa Markham. Is Dr. Warren there?"

She waited again, and then the president's deep voice came across the line.

"Melissa," he boomed, "glad to hear from you! I'm all set for New York. I got that packet of materials you sent over."

She took a deep breath. "Actually, Dr. Warren, there's something else I think I need to talk to you about. Could you fit in an appointment sometime tomorrow?"

There was a groan at the other end of the line. "Why does everything urgent happen the week before Christmas? I'm sorry, Melissa, but it'll just have to wait until after the holidays. My family's coming with me to New York, and we're going on to New England for a couple of weeks after Christmas. It'll be my first vacation in eighteen months."

Melissa smiled sympathetically. "I understand," she said, "but I think you'll want to know about this. It's important."

"Everything's important, Melissa." It was the first time she had ever heard Warren sound impatient. "I'm afraid there's just no time. Schedule something with Donna for right after I get back, okay? That's the best I can do."

Melissa sighed and tapped one of the piles on her desk with a pencil. "Okay," she said. "Anyway, that'll give me more time to go through the material I want to show you and get a real report together."

"Good girl," the president said. "Say," he added, his tone jovial once again, "whatever happened with that fellow Quarry? I meant to ask you about it after the game a couple weeks ago. He never did get up to watch the football, did he?"

"I don't think he really likes football," Melissa answered with a nervous laugh. "But he seemed to enjoy the party."

She hesitated a moment. Here's your opening, she told herself. Might as well plunge in.

"Actually, that's another thing I wanted to talk to you about," she went on. "I'm finding him . . . very difficult. I just can't seem to get a handle on him. I think maybe I should turn him over to you. Or Phil Donlon." Melissa could feel her cheeks growing warm as she spoke, and she had to reach for every single word; they seemed to keep bouncing just out of range.

There was a noticeable pause at the other end of the line, and Melissa ran a tongue between her dry lips.

"Well," Warren finally responded, "we'll talk about that after the holidays as well. Whatever's bothering you." He cleared his throat. "That fellow could certainly be a help to us, and not just in terms of money. He's getting quite a national reputation. Lots of good publicity. Quarry could push a lot of other people into helping out, if he'd come into the fold himself."

Melissa nodded mutely. I get the point, she thought impatiently. As if I needed any more pressure.

"Right?" the president boomed.

"Right," she agreed quietly. "We'll talk about it after the holidays. Have a nice vacation."

She hung up the receiver, feeling vaguely defeated. Then, with a deep breath, she stacked the three piles of papers on top of each other. She glanced around at the other work on her desk, but somehow it suddenly seemed irrelevant. With a sense of heaviness deep inside, she began to read the top page in the thick stack, making notes now and then on a pad at her elbow. As she read, she shook her head in disbelief.

Jeff had disappeared into his office while she was on the phone, and Melissa looked up, startled out of her concentration, when he eventually returned with a stack of morning mail in his hand.

"We're actually getting responses on the Christmas letters," he said with enthusiasm. He held up a fan of four or five letters.

"And then," he added, "there's this." He laid a cream-colored envelope on the desk in front of her. The return address, enclosed in a stylized lightning bolt logo, was in Elgin. But the postmark, Melissa noted as she ripped it open, was Chicago. On Saturday.

She pulled out a single sheet of lined paper. Almost unconsciously, she read it aloud. "Dear Ms. Markham, Thank you for your company this afternoon. I hope the enclosed will be an appropriate fee for your services thus far. Yours, Dakin Quarry."

Her eyes widened as she looked in the envelope again and pulled out a second enclosure—a check for two hundred and fifty dollars. She crumpled the check in her hand and threw it hard onto her desk. She could feel an almost physical flood of rage race through her body.

"I don't believe this!" she shouted, furious. "Who the hell does he think——" Then she looked up, suddenly aware that Jeff still stood across the desk from her.

"Two hundred and fifty dollars," she said more quietly. "From Mr. Dakin Quarry."

Jeff stared at her.

Terrific! she exploded at herself. So now Jeffrey knows there's something going on here, too. It's not enough you should kiss the guy in front of Bob Rudge. Go ahead, try and get out of it.

"From a man who's worth millions," she added lamely in an attempt to explain her anger. "I'll get two hundred and fifty *thousand* from Mr. Quarry before I'm through, no matter *what* it takes."

Jeff nodded thoughtfully, then reached out and picked up the check. He pressed it flat against the desk, carefully caressing the wrinkles out of it. "Well," he said mildly, "this is a beginning."

As soon as Jeff had left the office, Melissa picked up the phone and called Dake. He was on the line in seconds.

"*Mr.* Quarry," she began, her voice rigid with the effort of control, "just who do you think you are, sending me a check for my *services?* How dare you imply that my company is for sale?" Her voice rose despite everything. "How dare you suggest that——"

"You're shouting, Mel," Dake interrupted mildly.

"I know I'm shouting!" she shouted. "I'm very angry. I've never been so insulted——"

"Here we go again." Dake's voice was a little louder. "While we're at it, how dare *you* play games with me? Just what was it you thought you were doing with Bob Rudge?"

"I wasn't doing a damn thing with——"

Suddenly Melissa felt like giggling. She broke off her

sentence and moved the receiver away from her mouth.

"What?" Dake shouted. "What the . . ."

She couldn't control the laughter. It burst out in one long ripple that took her breath entirely away. She let herself dissolve with it.

There was a silence at the other end of the line.

"Mel?" Dake asked finally, his voice a little hesitant. "You okay?"

Melissa nodded and gasped for breath. "I'm sorry," she whispered. "I—" She gulped in air and let it out slowly. "It just suddenly seemed so silly," she said slowly. "We've seen each other—what? three times? I mean, I really hardly know you. And here I am, wasting this huge emotional blowout on you."

It was Dake's turn to laugh. "We were getting a little intense, weren't we? But I might dispute the argument that you don't *know* me. In the biblical sense—"

"You know what I mean," she interrupted quickly. "You know exactly what I mean. But sending that check was really a low blow."

"Yeah. Want one more of my patented apologies? I did it right after you stormed off on Saturday. I had that envelope stuck in my coat pocket, for some reason. I put the thing in the mailbox right there at the Watertower. I was angry as hell. I regretted it all day yesterday. But the post office is very uncooperative about retrieving such things."

"Well, I hope you suffered the full twenty-four hours. It was most offensive."

"I know." His voice was gentle again. "I'm sorry." He was silent for a moment. "Mel, how about a weekend off by ourselves? Somewhere we're guaranteed privacy. Just us."

Melissa sighed. "I don't see how that'll resolve anything, Dake." But even as she said the words, anticipation was running through her body, lighting tiny fires in every nerve ending. "I think we've got to figure this out with all the pieces included."

"Sometime," he agreed. "But first let's try to simplify

things a little. I want to know exactly what kind of exchanges you and Bob Rudge have had about me. About us. And I want to talk about it somewhere where there's no chance that Rudge will see you kissing me and draw his own conclusions."

"Me kissing *you!"* Melissa stuck her tongue out at the phone. "Anyway, you of all people know what kind of man Bob Rudge is. How could you possibly imagine me in collusion with him?"

"That's no explanation," Dake said calmly.

Melissa felt her impatience expanding. "I don't need to explain—"

She stopped, reminding herself sharply that *she* knew what kind of man Rudge was, too, especially after reading five pages of the material Jeff had gathered. But she had been ready to accept his explanation of why Dake had left school.

"Maybe we do need to talk things out," she said after a moment. "I have some questions that need answering, too. But I can only spare a day. It's very busy here."

"And a night," he answered softly, his voice a caress.

Melissa frowned at the receiver in her hand. Come on, Markham, don't do this to yourself. The man has possibly lied to you, and God knows he's wreaking havoc with your job.

But you love him, she added without thinking. You love him.

"Give me directions," she agreed. "I'll come out to your place after work on Friday."

It was almost seven when Melissa pulled her old green Pontiac into the driveway of Dake's restored nineteenth-century farmhouse. He was waiting at the front door with a duffel bag in his hand.

Melissa climbed out of her car. "I thought we were staying here," she said, pointing at the duffel.

Dake stepped out onto the front walk and pulled the door of the house shut behind him. He shook his head.

"I decided it should be neutral ground. Not yours, not mine."

He scooped Melissa's overnight bag from the back seat of her car and deposited it in the trunk of his Fiat. She watched, arms folded in front of her.

"Where'd you have in mind?" she asked as he gestured her into the front seat.

"North," he answered flatly.

The snow on the ground grew progressively deeper and whiter as they drove toward the Wisconsin border. Melissa sat curled in her seat, and as the softly veiled countryside moved by the window, she felt her tension fade slowly, as if the snow somehow muted everything, made it gentle. Ransom seemed very far away.

Sunlight had long since disappeared when the road they were on began following the shoreline of a large lake. Dake rounded the end of it and headed east.

Melissa sat up with a smile. "Lake Geneva," she said.

Dake grinned at her. "Fair?" he asked.

She nodded. "I always wanted to come here when I was married to Sandy. But he always wanted sun. He wouldn't consider any vacation that didn't involve lying on a beach."

Dake smiled. "Sounds like somebody deposited Sandy in the wrong place when they dropped him off in Chicago," he said lightly.

Melissa nodded. "I love the snow," she said. "It was one of many things Sandy and I didn't have in common."

Eventually Dake pulled the green Fiat into a lane that wound between two high snowbanks down toward the moonlit lake. Set way back on either side of the narrow road were log cottages, mere shadows in the dark night. Curls of smoke rose from the chimneys of two or three. Dake pulled into the cleared space in front of a larger building just at the lakeshore.

The night was velvety black, but the white moonlight reflected off the icy sheen of the lake with a brilliance that made everything luminescent. Melissa stood by the car and gazed at the frozen water while Dake went into the big lodge to get the key to their cabin.

"Over there," he said, emerging with the key and a piece of paper in his hand. He waved toward a cottage partway up the hill and well off the plowed road. A reassuring trail of gray smoke rose from its chimney.

"We have to leave the car here," Dake said, opening the trunk, "but they've shoveled a path and lit the fire."

Melissa glanced around. Except for two other cars parked nearby, the complex looked deserted.

"I brought some stuff," Dake went on. He handed Melissa their two overnight bags, then picked up a large cardboard box, balanced it on the back bumper, and slammed the trunk shut. "Let's head out."

Melissa stood looking at him for a moment longer. The moonlight gave his dark face the mystery she had seen there before—his eyes buried in shadow, the planes of his high cheeks and broad forehead reflecting the soft, gleaming light.

"Dake," she said finally, "thank you. This is beautiful." Her voice was soft with awe.

Dake nodded, his grin seeming to stretch from one ear to the other. "I know. All part of my master plan."

They trudged up the narrow path to the cabin, and Melissa unlocked the door and pushed it open with a sigh of relief. Warmth from the fire rushed out at them.

"Whoo! It's cold out there," she said as Dake followed her in, stamping snow off his feet on the small front porch.

The cabin was sparsely furnished but comfortable, with rag rugs and a huge overstuffed sofa in front of a blazing fireplace. Melissa unwound her muffler and shrugged off her down coat.

"I'm starving," she admitted, trailing after Dake as he carried the box of supplies into the alcove that served as a kitchen.

"Meat," he said gruffly, holding up two perfect strip steaks. "And potatoes." He pulled two potatoes wrapped in tin foil out of the box and handed them to Melissa. "Stick these in the fire, will you?"

Her face fell. "It'll take at least an hour for these to bake," she murmured. "Maybe—"

"They're almost done already," Dake answered. "I baked them for an hour at home. So they really just need to get heated up in the fire."

Melissa looked at him for a moment and shook her head, then walked over to the fire and tucked the potatoes in among the hot coals. "You think of everything," she said over her shoulder.

"Mmm." He had figured out how to work the grill, and he lit it with a flourish. "Dinner in fifteen minutes," he said. Then he turned and looked at Melissa with eyebrows raised. "Want to slip into something more comfortable?"

She laughed. "I think I'll stick to what I've got on, thank you very much."

They tossed a salad, and Dake uncorked the first of two bottles of wine he had brought along. He set a foil-wrapped loaf of buttered garlic bread on the hearth to warm while Melissa hunted for cutlery and plates in the kitchen drawers and cabinets and laid them out on the small table in front of the fire.

The cabin was toasty from the fire and the grill. The small windows were clouded over from the heat, and Melissa rubbed a palm against one, clearing a circle in its center. Outside, snow had started falling again. She watched it for a while, entranced. She felt a warmth inside, a sense of comfort that she knew was only partly due to the coziness of the cabin and the glass of wine in her hand. She sat on the couch in front of the fire and watched Dake as he forked the steaks off the grill and onto plates.

His lean body was outlined by the single light in the kitchen alcove, and Melissa could sense rather than see the play of his muscles as he moved around the tiny room. He wore thick corduroy work pants—the first time she had seen him in anything but jeans—and a plaid flannel shirt over a red cotton turtleneck. The shirt sleeves were rolled up, his bronze forearms covered by a soft golden down.

"You know," she said thoughtfully, "I can't remember a single time Sandy actually cooked for me."

"Men should do more of that." Dake whistled softly as he pulled the bread from the coals. His hands moved quickly, salting the steaks sparingly, adding the salt and a tub of butter to the tray he now brought over to the table. He leaned over to put the tray down, and the dancing firelight caught his face for a moment.

Melissa felt her breath quicken, and she shifted against the couch. Her body felt simultaneously light and heavy—ready to float into the circle of his strong arms, and yet filled with a heavy, liquid heat that signaled her readiness for his love. She lowered her head in embarrassed confusion.

"Ready to eat?" he asked.

She nodded. Dake retrieved the potatoes from the fire and served the salad. The aromas of the food were seductive, and suddenly Melissa realized again how hungry she was. It was, after all, well after nine o'clock at night, and she hadn't eaten since lunch. She took a bite of the tender steak and sighed with pleasure.

"Good?" he asked, chewing on a mouthful himself.

Melissa nodded. She scooped out a steaming mound of potato, dripping with butter, and let it cool for a moment before putting it in her mouth. When the butter trickled down her chin, Dake leaned forward and licked away the tiny trail, then wiped it carefully with his napkin.

Firelight prismed through their crystal wineglasses, making the rich burgundy sparkle with tiny, dancing pinpoints of light. It seemed to Melissa that she had never been happier in all her life.

When they had finished, they pushed the table away and lay back against the couch, watching the fire. Dake twined his fingers through Melissa's, and she could feel the trembling begin again where he touched her.

"You said on the phone that you had questions to ask," he said after several moments of silence.

Melissa blinked. She had pushed her doubts about Dake so far down into herself that she could hardly retrieve them. She sat up a little straighter, but she left her hand in his.

"Well," she began, "I guess I do. But you start. You wanted to know about Rudge and me."

Dake's smile faded. "I just want an explanation for what he did last Saturday."

Melissa nodded. "Okay. He's made it clear to me that you were always . . . interested in a pretty face. And that his idea of my doing my job properly would involve using that interest of yours to Ransom's advantage."

Dake's eyes were steady on her face. "But you threw him out of your office?"

Melissa sighed. "Yes," she answered flatly. "Whatever I feel for you has nothing to do with my job. But there isn't much I can do to stop him from thinking that I'm following his advice—except stop seeing you altogether."

Bob Rudge. It all came back to him, Melissa told herself. She'd give anything not to have to mention his name for the next twenty-four hours.

Dake nodded slowly. "Okay. Finally I see your problem. And I refuse to let his salacious ideas ruin a relationship I'm starting to like a lot. But you have to realize it's not easy for me, Mel. It's been fifteen years, and I still live by some of the rules he taught me."

He shifted slightly and crossed one leg over the other, beginning to massage the calf with his free hand. "So now, your turn. What questions?"

Melissa rubbed her brow. "Well, I'm afraid this is about Rudge, too. The thing is, I went to see him, to ask about all the things you said. About how scholarship athletes are treated and all that." The words came out in a rush, almost tumbling over one another. Dake's hand held hers, but Melissa sensed a new stiffness in it. She turned her face to look at him anxiously.

"He wouldn't say much, but I mentioned it to my secretary, Jeff," she went on, "and he compiled a file on the athletic department that's enough to curl your hair." She could hear the eagerness in her voice. "It's just incredible, Dake, what he's been getting away with all this time."

Dake's dark eyes were steady on her face. "What questions?" he said quietly. "You can tell me the rest of this later. What questions did you need to ask me?"

Melissa looked back at the fire and pressed her lips together. She really didn't care anymore, she knew, why Dake had left Ransom. But she didn't want to know that he had lied to her.

"Rudge says you left school to play pro basketball in Italy. Not because you couldn't afford it anymore. He says your poor-little-farm-boy story is pure fairy tale."

Dake dropped her hand and rose abruptly. He put both hands on the mantel for a moment, then turned and faced Melissa, one hand still resting on the fireplace.

"And you believed him," he said dully.

Melissa felt something race through her that she knew was fear—fear of losing the man she loved. "He had a magazine article," she said defensively.

Dake shook his head sadly. "I told you I'd played basketball in Europe. You *knew* that. Why would you believe him and not me?"

She blinked away the first hint of a tear. *"You* believed him," she whispered. "About me. And anyway, the timing was so close..."

Dake straightened his shoulders sharply, as if shaking off a sudden chill. "Okay," he said. "I left Ransom for exactly the reasons I told you." His voice was without emotion, and the words came wearily, as if he had been through this one too many times. "I was broke. My family was broke. When I got back to Colorado, I spent about a month on the farm, and that was hell for everybody. I didn't want to be there, and my parents were so depressed it was killing them. They felt they'd let me down; they couldn't give me the education they wanted me to have."

He stared at the floor for a moment, then looked back at Melissa. His gaze seemed vaguely accusing, as if she had somehow had something to do with his parents' disappointment. "They wanted me to graduate from college. So I went over to State in Fort Collins to register and see if they were still interested in offering me anything for my talents. Another deal," he added.

Melissa took a pillow from the couch and pressed it against her stomach. She nodded.

"I ran into a guy I'd played basketball against in high school. He was heading for Italy to play ball. He suggested I come along. He had me talk with this recruiter, and we played some pick-up ball for him, and I signed a contract. I left three weeks later."

"What about college?" Melissa asked. "What about your parents?"

Dake pressed his lips together for a moment before he continued, as if holding in an emotion stronger than he wanted to express. "My parents had put everything they had into my one extra semester at Ransom. With the bad harvest, they were pretty close to bankrupt. I needed money a whole lot more than I needed a degree right then."

His voice was tight and bitter, and Melissa watched him with wide, sympathetic eyes. Dake took his hand off the mantel and paced back and forth.

"I played for Turin. Fiat city," he added with a small smile.

Melissa smiled back at him, grateful for his expression.

"I was good enough that they tore up my contract after a couple of months," he went on, "and renegotiated. I started making a whole lot of money. I bailed out my parents, and I started piling some up for myself."

"But you were injured," Melissa said. She wanted to believe everything, she wanted Dake to be perfect, but she could hear the small note of accusation in her voice.

He glanced at her sharply. "I *told* Rudge I'd be ready to run again by then. This was a whole year after the injury, remember."

He took another couple of steps, then stopped. "Anyway, I'd designed this special shoe with a particular insert in the heel that really seemed to spread the pressure around. I figured it out when I was working at the shoe factory. I had some made up for me, and the tendon seemed okay for the most part after that." He shrugged. "I had them made for the other guys on the team in Italy, too."

The smile flickered across his face again, and this time it was a little wider. "I played for twelve years, got married briefly to an Italian model, and put enough money in the bank to come back here and buy my factory. I've been manufacturing my special shoe ever since. End of story."

Melissa watched him. The fire jumped and crackled behind him, and she was struck again by the width of his shoulders, the raw strength of his body.

"It sounds very tidy," she said.

Dake nodded with a wry smile. "Very tidy," he agreed. "Very neat. Except that I never got the college degree. Which happened to be the one thing I really wanted. My parents never quite got over that disappointment. I don't think I'll ever forgive Bob Rudge for that."

"You could go back," Melissa said earnestly. "You could have gone back any time, once you had the money." She was smiling at him. He hadn't lied. He wanted nothing from her, no revenge; he wanted her for herself alone.

Dake shook his head slowly. "I know it sounds cranky, but I wanted a *Ransom* degree, Mel. And they're not big on thirty-six-year-old students."

He took two steps toward Melissa and stood towering in front of her. Then suddenly he seemed to collapse toward her, only his hands on the back of the couch preventing his big body from covering hers. "Enough," he said. "We've got dishes to do."

He leaned forward a little more and brought his mouth to hers. He nibbled tenderly at her lips. Melissa let her head drop back against the couch and closed her eyes. She felt safe, enclosed within the circle of his arms, his lips gentle on her face.

"Mmm," he murmured after a moment. "Garlic."

The pressure of his mouth grew harder. For a moment longer, only their mouths touched. Then Melissa slid her hands around his waist and pulled him against her. He lifted his hands from the back of the couch and buried one in the thickness of her hair. He was kneeling now, as he had at her apartment in front of her chair, but abruptly he rose. Melissa's eyes opened wide.

Dake stood in front of her. The fire outlined his body with its sparkling light, and his movements were full of grace as he leaned and scooped her up in his arms. She could feel the tense, corded muscles of his arms around her; she stroked his shoulder hesitantly, as she might stroke the flank of a cat long familiar but just returned from a week's disappearance. It was hard to assess what wildness had been learned in those days away.

Melissa lay back in his arms as he carried her through the open doorway into the bedroom. It was a small room, with two curtained windows, an old wooden dresser, a single chair, and a double bed that took up most of its space. Dake had to maneuver his way between the bed and the wall to lay Melissa gently onto the chenille spread.

He sat down beside her, and she stretched, catlike, rubbing her head against his hip. He stroked her hair gently.

Then suddenly they were both in motion, their hands guided by an urgency that was as powerful as it was new. Melissa fumbled with the buttons on his shirt, muttering as her fingers first failed and then finally succeeded in their task. She pulled the shirt off, then slipped his turtleneck over his head. Dake struggled with Melissa's butter-yellow sweater until finally she pulled it off herself, tossing it onto the dresser just a few feet away.

They rose and stood together in the narrow space beside the bed just long enough to slide their slacks down onto the floor; then Melissa burrowed beneath the several layers of covers on the bed. The room, she noticed for the first time, was cold.

Dake nestled beside her in the cocoon of blankets, his chest pressed against her back. She could feel the pounding of his heart; it threatened, it seemed to her, to break her vertebrae with the strength of its beating. And lower, against the soft flesh of her thighs, she could feel the hardness of him throbbing, ready.

He slid a hand beneath her and covered one firm breast with it, his strong, gentle fingers kneading the tender flesh, brushing its taut center, teasing the nipple until it stood erect. His other hand slipped over her hip to seek the chestnut-colored down beneath her belly and buried itself there. Melissa heard herself moan softly. She started to turn, but Dake held her against him for a moment longer, her back to his broad chest, until Melissa felt she would burst with the agony of anticipation.

"Please, Dake," she breathed, "oh, please!"

He relaxed the strength of his hands and let her turn toward him, then pulled her quickly onto him. Melissa felt like some wild thing, some jungle animal; she twisted above him as great waves of desire shook her whole body; she pulled at his thick hair and bit his shoulder.

Then finally she buried her face in the hollow of his neck as his body began to move rhythmically beneath her, first gently, then more quickly. The movements of his body grew larger, more expansive, until she could feel him deep inside her, taking more than she had ever willingly given before.

She cried out once, then again, as the sweet agony of it all overwhelmed her, and she struggled for a moment against Dake's arms. But after he reached his own shuddering release, he held her with a tender strength, soothing her wildness, making her acknowledge the completeness of their union.

"Okay?" he asked after several breathless moments.

Melissa nodded, and Dake shifted her body so that she slipped off his chest and lay snuggled against him in the now-warm cocoon of the bed.

"Mmm," she said.

He laughed and ran a finger down her cheek, then around her ear. He brought his face to hers and brushed her eyelids and the tip of her nose with his lips. Melissa shivered in delight.

"Can we stay here forever?" she asked, her voice husky with pleasure and exhaustion.

Dake laughed again. "Check-out is noon tomorrow," he said. "And we've still got dishes to do!"

Melissa nuzzled his chest. "Mmm," she murmured again. She kissed the subtle rise of muscle around his nipples, then the flat plane of his belly. She slid her hands around him and let them explore his back—the powerful muscles and sinews, the hard edges of his shoulders.

Dake shifted and said a little hoarsely, "Mel, we really should clean up from dinner..."

But an hour later, when Dake finally climbed out of the bed and disappeared into the kitchen, Melissa was only dimly aware of his absence. She lay back against the pillows, smiling, satisfied, ready for sleep.

- 8 -

THE NEXT THING Melissa was conscious of was the enticing aroma of bacon frying. When she lifted her head, she could hear it crackling as well. Hesitantly, she opened first one eye and then the other, and she took a moment as she breathed in the delicious odor to remember exactly where she was. She rolled over onto her side, and her body felt tender and just a bit strange to her.

Oh, yes, she told herself with a catlike stretch and a small smile. Dake.

But his half of the bed was empty.

"Dake?" she called.

He appeared in the doorway almost immediately, a dish towel tucked into the waistband of his corduroy pants. He was grinning.

"Morning, Mel."

Melissa stretched again and smiled. "Breakfast ready?" she asked lazily.

Dake laughed out loud. "You look like a kitten. A long-haired kitten. Food in five minutes." He turned and disappeared.

Melissa slid one leg tentatively out from under the warm covers. The room was chilly; the warmth of the fire didn't extend quite far enough. Her foot touched the icy plank floor, and she pulled it quickly back under the covers. With the blanket held tightly under her chin, she sat up and looked around.

Dake had brought their bags in from the living room, and he had put hers down on the floor within easy reach. On top of it sat a pair of heavy woolen socks—his, no doubt. Melissa leaned out of bed, scooped up the canvas overnight bag, and pulled it under the blanket with her.

With awkward motions, the covers forming a tent over her head, she began to dress. The socks were toasty warm and just a little scratchy. She unzipped the bag and picked out the change of clothes she had brought—jeans, a turtleneck, and her heavy Irish sweater. Then, hesitantly, she pushed the covers back and tested the floor again.

"It's warmer in here," Dake called from the other room as if he could see through the wall. "And it's easier if you run."

Melissa made a dash for the living room. The fire was roaring, and the warmth came at her with a comforting rush. She pulled up in front of the fireplace and rubbed her hands together.

Dake looked at her. He was standing by the stove, spatula in hand, scrambling eggs. He nodded in approval.

"Always liked that sweater," he said a little smugly.

Melissa shot him a coy smile, remembering how his strong hands had pulled it over her head when they had made love the first time.

"Bathroom's through there," he added, pointing with the spatula to a door as he turned his attention back to the eggs.

Melissa nodded and headed over to the bathroom. She pulled the door shut behind her and proceeded to wash away any remaining traces of sleep. She tried to tame her hair in front of the mirror, pushing and pulling at the springy auburn curls that framed her face, but it seemed pretty much a hopeless cause. Despairingly, she tucked it behind her ears.

When she returned to Dake's side, he was dishing out

eggs. She sniffed in approval.

"It smells wonderful," she said.

They shared the eggs and bacon, bagels buttered and heated in the coals, orange juice, and strong coffee. Melissa felt as if she had been deprived of food for a week and now was eating for the first time; everything tasted fresh and sweet, and she could hardly get enough.

The morning sun shone brilliant and white through the windows, touching the inside of the small cabin with an almost magical sparkle. Outside, the whole world seemed to glitter with snow and sunlight. There was, she sighed softly to herself, no trouble in paradise.

Maybe Dake's right, she thought as she washed dishes after the meal and deposited them back in cupboards. Maybe we *are* perfect for each other—as long as it's just the two of us, somewhere far away and absolutely isolated.

She smiled ruefully. Hard to live that way all the time, though.

When the dishes were done, they pulled on jackets and mufflers and gloves and pushed each other out into the foot-deep snow. They built a snowman.

"We'll call him Coach," Dake said as Melissa packed more and more snow around the figure's already stout middle. "And leave him to melt in the sun."

Melissa giggled and added another chin.

They trudged down to the lake and threw pebbles at the icy skim on the surface. Some bounced off; some broke through and sank to the bottom. Melissa made silent wishes whenever a pebble disappeared through the ice.

They threw snowballs at each other. Melissa shoved a handful of snow down the back of Dake's jacket, and he pulled her down into the powdery stuff and rubbed her face in it.

"No fair," she sputtered, licking the flakes off her mouth. "You're bigger than I am. I should have a handicap."

"You do. You're smarter," Dake called as he tossed

a handful of snow on top of her. She lay back and made an angel.

They kissed. Dake's mouth felt icy cold, but its touch brought a warmth to her body that made Melissa want to pull off all the layers of down and wool that separated her from him.

After an hour, clothes soaked through, they headed inside. Melissa changed from her jeans back to the pants she had worn the day before, and she spread her jacket and gloves in front of the fire to dry.

"Almost noon," Dake called from the alcove kitchen. "Check-out time."

A few minutes later Melissa reluctantly got up from where she had been kneeling in front of the fireplace. She pulled her slightly damp jacket back on, picked up the two bags, and followed Dake down the narrow shoveled path to the car. She was quiet as they stowed their bags in the trunk.

If they could do this once a month forever, she decided, she could be happy.

But even as the thought passed through her mind, she shook her head. No, she'd want more. And as soon as they got back to civilization, their whole beautiful, perfect little ice castle would probably melt away.

Dake touched her arm. "Ready to go?"

She looked up at him. The chilly air had ruddied his bronze cheeks, and his hair gleamed dark against the brilliant white snow. Melissa's gaze swept up and down his lanky body. He raised both hands and pushed his hair off his forehead with spread fingers.

I love him. It was a notion that had come before, just as abruptly, but this time it settled in her heart, and she realized that it had been there all along. I love him. But I can never really have him.

She turned away. "Yep," she said as lightly as she could manage, slamming the trunk shut. "Ready to go."

They drove the long way around this time, at Dake's insistence. "Got something I want you to see," he said mysteriously as he pulled off the road a few miles from the cabin into the parking lot of a small roundish building covered by an immense dome.

"Yerkes Observatory," he said with a wave of his hand. "I came up here with an astronomy class from Ransom. I've always been fascinated by this stuff."

Melissa looked at him curiously. Mr. Dakin Quarry was ever surprising. Most surprising indeed.

Inside, an intense, bearded young man who seemed to recognize Dake showed them the great telescope, big as a prehistoric dinosaur, and Melissa could feel Dake's excitement. The astronomer set in motion a massive piece of machinery that uncovered the dome and the lens of the telescope, and he showed them how the lens could be turned.

"It feels like Wonderland," Melissa whispered to Dake with a laugh.

The young man stopped talking and looked at her sternly, but Dake grinned.

"Yeah. Everything's the wrong size," he said. "All out of scale. I think that's what I like, too. That, and the fact that stars follow patterns, rules. They can't disappoint you, the way people can."

He took her hand and held it tightly as they left the observatory.

"You know who you were?" Melissa asked as they climbed back into the car.

Dake looked at her quizzically. "What do you mean, who I was?"

"In Wonderland."

His gaze remained cloudy for a moment and then suddenly cleared. "Oh, yeah! Like the White Rabbit and Alice. No, who?"

"The Cheshire Cat," Melissa said, turning in her seat to look at him as he started the car. "You sort of appear and disappear. And sometimes all that's left is your smile, suspended in the air."

Dake looked at her a moment longer, then nodded

thoughtfully. The Fiat's engine turned over a little painfully in the cold. Melissa waited—waited for him to say something about never disappearing again. Waited for him to say that they could overcome any obstacles, even Ransom College. Even Bob Rudge. But he didn't. He just backed the car out of the observatory parking lot and headed for the main road. Finally, a tiny sadness taking root inside her, Melissa turned away.

They stopped in Lake Geneva Village for hamburgers, and they pulled back into Dake's driveway at a little after three o'clock.

"Come on in," he said as Melissa headed around the car to the trunk to retrieve her bag. "Have some hot chocolate or something."

She smiled. "It's been wonderful, Dake," she said softly. "But . . ."

His eyes widened in little-boy cajolery. "Oh, come on, Mel. What's one cup of hot chocolate?" His tone was low and compelling, and Melissa spread her hands in defeat.

"Okay. But just one. I'd like to see your house."

They shifted her bag to her own car, then went inside. As soon as they were through the door, Dake kicked off his boots and tossed them into a basket on the floor. Beside it, lined up neatly, were three pairs of Windflame shoes. Melissa smiled as she pulled off her own boots and pushed them to one side of the entrance hall.

The house was comfortably warm. It was also, Melissa noted with an interested eye, simply beautiful—perfectly restored to its nineteenth-century charm, with dark wood against white plaster, wide-board floors, and multi-paned windows set deep into thick walls. It had clearly never been an elegant house, but it had a soft patina of loveliness to it that only age and tender care could bring.

She wandered slowly around the first floor as Dake heated milk in the kitchen. A large parlor opened onto a bright-yellow dining room, and on the other side of the entry hall, a library had pride of place—a small, cozy room crammed full with floor-to-ceiling bookcases. Every room had a fireplace.

"Not bad for a bankrupt farmer," Melissa said wryly as she joined Dake in the kitchen. She glanced around at the sparkling white cabinets and the pine floor.

He shrugged, pouring hot milk from a saucepan, and plopping tiny marshmallows into two pottery mugs. "I like it. It was falling down when I found it a couple of years ago. I've done some of the work myself. I like things simple."

"Simple but perfect," Melissa added.

He smiled as he handed her a mug. Then he planted a kiss on the tip of her nose. "Or complex but perfect," he said.

Melissa raised her eyebrows, and Dake shrugged. "Like telescopes," he added. He slid an arm around her shoulders. "Want to see the rest of the house?"

Melissa nodded, but she wrapped both hands around the warm mug and stepped away a little. There had to be an end to this sometime.

"Upstairs," he said. He took a big sip of hot chocolate and scooped out a marshmallow, now melted almost to foam, with his tongue. Then he put the mug down. "Come and see it all. The bedrooms, too."

He took her hand and led her through the kitchen and up the narrow back stairs. A hallway opened onto two bedrooms—a small guest room above the library and a large one with a fireplace above the main parlor. An intricate quilt covered the big bed in the larger room, and a second, in soft earth tones, hung on the wall.

Melissa stood in the doorway of the room and looked around. "The quilts are gorgeous," she said.

Dake slipped an arm over her shoulders again. "My mother, the quilter," he said with a note of pride in his voice. "Someday you'll have to show me some of your mom's weavings."

A desk occupied one corner of the room, and more

books were strewn here and there and piled up on the bedside table, even on the floor. Melissa glanced at the titles: biographies, histories, contemporary fiction.

"Well," she said, gesturing at the books, "Ransom must have taught you to read, at least."

Dake laughed. "Not Ransom. I always loved to read. But some of my professors did point me in the right direction, I have to admit."

Dake started into the room, his arm still draped comfortably around Melissa's shoulders, but she stood firm in the doorway, refusing the pressure. He turned to look at her.

"Mel," he said softly, "stay the night. We can shut out the world here." His fingers traced a small circle on her upper arm, and Melissa felt the familiar shivers begin again. Her mug of chocolate trembled in her hand.

She shook her head firmly. "No. We can't shut the world out. Not forever." She stepped away from him. "I've got work, and anyway, the deal was one night."

"Deal?" he echoed, eyebrows raised.

Melissa grimaced. "Bad choice of words. Sorry. But I've got other commitments."

He shook his head. "No," he said. "I'm busy, too. I want a serious excuse."

Melissa looked at him for a moment, then took his free hand in hers. "Dake, please don't do this to me. I'm confused. I want to be with you, but I just don't see how we can ignore the realities of my world. Of my job. Either you have to figure out how to accommodate Ransom in your feelings for me, or there can't be anything more between us."

Okay, Markham, you've said it. Now it's up to him.

Dake swung her hand lightly, like a small child might, as he looked at her.

"Okay," he said after a moment. "You want me to make room for Ransom? You got it. Come on downstairs. I want to tell you something."

He led her down to the library and settled her into the

big leather chair there, then busied himself for a moment
building a fire. When the flames caught, he stood up,
brushed off his hands, and moved over to the window.
He leaned back against the ledge, his arms folded over
his chest. The faded colors of his flannel shirt took on
a new brightness from the sun glancing through the window.

"I've been back in Chicago for about three years," he
said finally. "And I've been thinking about Ransom on
and off that whole time. What it did for me. What I
learned there. You're right, you know: Ransom got me
out of where I was and showed me all kinds of new
things." He waved a hand in the air and smiled. "Telescopes, for instance.

"My business has made a whole lot more money than
I ever expected. When I started the company, I figured
we'd be making shoes for pros—you know, serious athletes who really had a stake in preventing injuries. But
for some reason, without even much in the way of ad-
vertising..."

Dake rolled his eyes and shrugged. "They've taken
off in the general market as well. We've had to expand
the plant twice, and this Christmas we're still struggling
to keep our stores stocked. It's nice, but it's really..."
He hesitated, and rubbed his forehead for a moment with
the tip of one finger. "It's really more than I need."

Melissa tilted her head to one side. "What about your
parents?" she asked. "Do they still need help?"

Dake smiled. "That was my first priority. Right now
they may be the only farmers in the entire country without
a single debt."

Melissa curled her feet under her in the big chair.
Looking at Dake, silhouetted by the light streaming
through the window behind him, she felt a surge of wanting him that was almost painful.

"So," he continued after a moment, "the point is, even
after debts and investments, I have all this money. And
a year or so ago, I began thinking that maybe..." He

unfolded his arms and pushed his hair back with spread fingers, then jammed his hands into his pockets. "Maybe I should give Ransom something. To help out kids like I was once."

Melissa shifted in the chair and let her eyes wander quickly around the room. Suddenly she didn't want to look at Dake anymore.

"You're not going to offer me money for my services again, are you?" she said, trying to keep her voice light.

She glanced at him long enough to see an expression of annoyance pass quickly over his face and disappear.

"No," he said curtly. "We're talking business now, Mel." He was quiet for a moment, until he caught Melissa's eye again and made her look steadily at him.

"Last spring I ran into an old teacher of mine downtown. Professor Goldman. English?"

Melissa nodded. "I know him," she said.

"He was one incredible teacher. I really enjoyed him. We both had places to get to, but we talked a little about Ransom. The money situation for scholarships and all that. I decided then it was time, so I took a hundred thousand dollars and put it into an escrow fund with my lawyer, to be transferred to Ransom in one year."

Melissa looked at him curiously. "Why not just donate the money outright? You could have earmarked it for student assistance or whatever you like."

Dake ducked his head, and when he looked up again, his smile was a little sheepish. "I was hedging my bets. The escrow was set up so the money would go to Ransom a year from the date it was deposited unless I gave my lawyer compelling evidence before then that Ransom wouldn't use it properly."

Melissa sat up abruptly. "You mean you didn't trust the college to—"

"Why should I?" Dake interrupted, a sudden edge to his voice. "My own experience wasn't very promising." He smiled again. "But in point of fact, after I set up the fund, I didn't do a damn thing more about it. I guess I subconsciously decided I didn't want to stir up old battles. I think I'd even half convinced myself that Rudge must be retired by now. So the money would have been donated next spring, sort of by default."

Melissa slid one hand along the smooth leather arm of the chair. "I sense a 'but' coming on," she said.

Dake turned away, his back to Melissa, and looked out the window. She could see his shoulders rise and fall as he breathed, and the straight cut of his black hair just below the collar of his flannel shirt touched her heart. She thought suddenly of when he had stalked out of the dinner that first night, so icy, so angry . . .

But when he turned back, he was smiling. "It was all your fault," he said. "When I laid eyes on you that first time, outside the museum restaurant, I decided that any institution that would hire somebody who looked like you must be okay. I almost went home and sent the money over that same day." His smile broadened. "Then it occurred to me that if I poked around a little—who knew? Maybe I'd run into Melissa Markham, director of development, sometime somewhere again."

The fire flickered and began to fade. Dake glanced at it, then moved over to the fireplace and stabbed at the charred logs with the poker. After a moment, the crackling flames rose again, and Dake moved back to the window. He took a couple of steps to one side of the window, then turned back again—pacing, the way he had in front of the fireplace the night before.

"Not very long after that, I found the dinner invitation in my mail. I went back and forth about it—I'm not big on social evenings like that. But at the last minute I decided to go." He stopped moving and clenched his fists at his sides. "And then the first thing that got tossed at me was that this stadium was going to be named after Robert Rudge."

Dake looked steadily at Melissa. "Mel, I thought I was over it. But I'd forgotten how much I despised that man."

Melissa nodded slowly. "But Rudge doesn't need to be involved in a donation from you," she said.

"Rudge doesn't need to be involved in Ransom College at all," Dake responded bitterly. His expression had hardened the same way it had at the dinner when Katherine McAllister mentioned the stadium; his eyes seemed to reflect the icy sheen on the snow outside the window.

"I'm prepared to offer Ransom five hundred thousand dollars, Mel, on the condition that you see to it that Robert Rudge is fired as athletic director."

Melissa rose from her chair. "What?" she cried.

Dake nodded, and there was a grim smile on his face. "Half a million dollars for scholarships, Mel. With only that one string attached. You get Rudge fired. You started to tell me last night that you have the ammunition."

Ammunition was a word Rudge had used, too. It was as though the two men thought of each other as prey—and she was somehow the weapon.

Melissa felt a terrible coldness inside; it began in the depths of her belly and moved slowly outward, through her legs and arms, into the tips of her fingers.

"Is that what this is all about?" she asked. Her voice was almost a whisper, invaded by the iciness inside. She remembered what she had wondered once before, if Dake was using her, if his bitterness was so strong . . .

"What what's all about?" he said. "It's a simple deal, Mel. The kind of thing that's done all the time."

Melissa took in a deep breath, but it seemed to freeze before it even reached her lungs.

"Not by me," she whispered. She cleared her throat, and when she continued, her voice was a little stronger. "Maybe I don't understand that kind of deal-making."

Dake slapped one hand down on the desk, and Melissa winced. "Come on. Try to understand my point of view. My parents wanted that Ransom degree more than anything in the world, Mel. So did I. He ruined my life," he said, his voice quiet. "Bob Rudge ruined my life."

A tiny spiral of anger coiled inside her. Melissa opened her eyes wide and looked pointedly around the lovely room. "It hardly looks like a ruin to me," she answered sharply. "In fact, it looks rather profitable."

Dake pressed his lips together but said nothing for a moment. Then he repeated the offer. "Five hundred thousand for Rudge's job, Mel. Take it or leave it."

Melissa lifted her hands off the arms of the chair, which she had been leaning on ever since she had pushed herself up. She stood as straight as she could manage, fighting against the cold and the anger inside her.

"Right this minute, Dake," she said finally, "I don't see how you're so terribly different from Bob Rudge. He wants me to sleep with you for a hundred thousand, and you want me to fire him for five hundred thousand. Well, I'll have to let you both down. I don't do deals. I really thought you understood that. No thanks—to both of you."

She turned and walked out of the room, pausing in the hallway only long enough to retrieve her jacket and boots before she stalked out of the house. Somehow the outdoors seemed warmer than the inside of her body, and it was comforting.

The drive home took less than an hour, and she played the radio loud the whole time, drowning out her thoughts.

Well, Melissa told herself as she pulled into a parking space outside her apartment, that's the end of that. With mechanical motions, she picked up her weekend bag from the back seat, locked the car, unlocked the downstairs door of the house, and clicked it shut again behind her.

The rooms at the top of the stairs looked exactly as they had the morning before, when she had left them; but Melissa felt that something had changed irrevocably.

She set her bag down in the bedroom, then turned on the hot water in the tub. Gingerly, as if her body were breakable, she pulled off her layers of sweaters, her slacks, her underwear. She stared for a moment at the heavy socks—Dake's socks—then dropped them out of sight into the laundry hamper.

She sank down into the big old claw-footed tub, leaving only her face above water. Slowly, the iciness in her fingers began to thaw, then in her arms and legs, and finally the warmth began to penetrate the rest of her body. Her cheeks felt hot to the touch, suddenly flushed from the heat of the water.

You'll get over him, she told herself firmly as her strength began to return; it just takes time. The phone began to ring as she rubbed shampoo into her hair. She started to rise from the tub, and water cascaded in little waterfalls off her thighs and belly. But then she thought better of it, and she let the phone go unanswered. It didn't ring again.

By Monday, the campus was almost deserted. Tuesday would be the last day of exams, and only a handful of students were still around. The layer of snow that had been in place for several weeks now was piled into gray mounds, alternately turning to slush at midday and back again to ice in the late afternoon.

It was a bad time for alumni contacts, right before Christmas, and plans for activities after the holidays were pretty much in hand. Melissa drafted a needed round of campaign pleas and then turned her full attention to Jeff's file on the athletic department.

It was remarkable, she thought again and again as she read through the material, that this had been allowed to go on for so long. She pulled out statistics, catalogued recruiting violations, then tried to make sense of all her notes before drafting her summary for President Warren.

She had long since told her parents that she would stay in Chicago for Christmas, and she had anticipated an invitation from the McAllisters. But when Katherine called on Wednesday just before noon, it was to tell her that she and Alan had decided to visit their daughter in Washington.

"Now you *are* going home, aren't you, Lissie?" Katherine asked a little anxiously.

Melissa shrugged. "I'm well taken care of," she responded. "You have a good time with Diane."

"Oh dear," Katherine said, instantly concerned. "You'd planned to come here, hadn't you? I feel just terrible!"

"Katherine, I am *not* your special charge," she said firmly. "I have lots of friends. I may still go home. Whatever I do, I'll enjoy it."

There was a brief pause. "Are you absolutely sure, Lissie? We'll be back right after Christmas. We'll call you then—I'm sure we'll want company."

"That would be great, Kath. I'll talk to you then if I'm in town. Merry Christmas."

"All right, dear," Katherine said, still concerned. "Merry Christmas to you. And from Alan. Bye now."

Melissa set the phone down gently and frowned. She wasn't sure what to do. She hated traveling during the holidays, but she and Sandy had always carefully alternated visiting first one set of parents and then the other. For the past two years, since her divorce, her parents had almost insisted that she spend the holidays with them.

This year she had been rather looking forward to a city Christmas, with the audience-participation *Messiah* at the Auditorium downtown, and the symphony's holiday concert. She supposed she could always beg a Christmas Day invitation from a friend, but she didn't much relish inviting herself somewhere . . . any more than she liked the idea of a turkey breast cooked in her own oven.

"Jeff?" she called through the open door to the outer office.

Jeff poked his head in.

"What're you doing for Christmas?" she asked. "Going home?"

He grinned and shook his head. "Nope. Susie's house this year," he said.

Melissa returned his smile. "A budding romance?"

He laughed. "Budding, hell. It's in full bloom. I'm going over to athletics now to pick her up for lunch. Want me to bring you back a sandwich?"

"Nope. I'll get something at the union."

"What about you?" he asked. "Going home for the holidays?"

Melissa shrugged. "Maybe so," she said. "I don't know."

She bundled into her down jacket and headed for the coffee shop at the student union, the only restaurant on campus still open. She was halfway there, staring at the sidewalk to avoid puddles and icy patches, when a loud voice roused her from her thoughts.

"Hey, darlin', daydreamin', are we?"

She glanced up at Bob Rudge's face, more florid than usual from the sub-freezing temperatures, and stopped walking. "Hi, Bob."

It was, she realized, the first time she had seen him since their encounter at Watertower Place. She viewed that incident, in retrospect, as the beginning of the end of her relationship with Dake. And it was inescapably clear now that Rudge had been a sticking point right from the start. She looked at him with narrowed eyes.

"What's been goin' on over there at the money shop?" he asked.

Suddenly, impulsively, Melissa wanted to strike back.

"Well," she said quietly, "we've been gathering a few things besides dollars lately, Bob. We've been gathering some information, too."

He smiled broadly. "I expect that's part of your job, ma'am. Part of everybody's. The world runs on information."

Melissa looked at his bright-red nose with distaste and nodded. "Yes, it does," she answered. "We happen to think it's a college's job to provide honest and admirable leadership for its students. It's hard to raise money for a place you don't trust to spend it properly."

Rudge was waving to someone across the quad, and

Melissa hesitated for a moment.

"Sorry," he said with a wink. "You were sayin' something about admiring your leaders?"

Melissa straightened her shoulders beneath the puffy down and nodded. "I was saying, it's hard to convince people to give money for special funds for athletes when those scholarship athletes are promised they won't have to work very hard for their grades as long as they perform on the football field."

Rudge's smile faded, and his blue eyes almost disappeared between folds of skin as he squinted at Melissa. "I'm not sure I'm following you, missy."

Melissa shrugged. "I think you should be, Bob."

Then suddenly Rudge's smile returned. "Why, I see," he said, wheezing from the cold. "You been cozying up with Mr. Dakin Quarry again. I do believe!" He laughed hard enough to make his whole frame shake. "Yes, I do believe so."

Melissa shook her head fiercely. "No. He was a victim of your lack of ethics, but only one."

"For a victim," Rudge said, "Mr. Quarry has certainly done rather well for himself. Yessir. Very well indeed."

Rudge leaned toward Melissa, and when he spoke again, his voice was lower. "And frankly, Miss Markham, I wonder if it's your right to be walkin' around makin' accusations about ethics and morals. I'm not sure Jack Warren would be real happy with your methods of fund-raising, if it comes down to that."

Melissa glared at him. "I don't know what you're talking about," she said sharply.

"I mean, if the president was aware just how seriously you've taken his instruction to reel in Mr. Quarry—I mean, just how *far* you've gone for that bit of money . . ."

"I don't know what you're talking about," Melissa repeated, but her voice sounded flat and mechanical.

"Oh, I think you do," Rudge breathed. "I do think you do." He stepped back and smiled again. "Now you have a nice Christmas, missy. I'll be in touch."

- 9 -

MELISSA SAT AT her desk, her head in her hands. She stared at the thick folder of information about the athletic department. On top of it rested her summary, an outline of the abuses of Robert Rudge's administration dating back almost twenty years.

Terrific, Markham, she told herself with a sigh. You've managed to paint yourself into the proverbial corner here. This stuff has to go on to the president. There's just no getting around that. But if it does . . .

She shook her head. It really didn't seem fair. She had been so meticulous about her conduct. She could tick off any number of fund-raisers whose ways and means of raising money didn't meet her own ethical standards. And yet, just because of Bob Rudge, it seemed likely that her job would be in jeopardy if—no, *when*— she handed the information in front of her over to President Warren.

She put both hands on top of the folder and stared at them, then glanced up at the sound of a soft tapping on her door.

"Boss?"

Melissa tried to smile as Jeff came into the office. "What's up?" she asked.

He blinked, stared at her for a moment, and ran a hand through his already rumpled hair.

"Boy," he said finally, "you look wiped out."

Melissa shrugged.

"Okay, none of my business." Jeff shifted his gaze to the window. "Anyway, you got a phone call while you were at lunch. Dake Quarry. He wants you to call back." He held a pink message slip toward her across the desk.

Melissa gazed at it for a moment, then suddenly snatched the paper out of his hand and ripped it in half. Jeff's brow furrowed in a little frown. Hesitantly, he retrieved the two pink pieces from the desk and held them in his hands, fitting them back together.

"Can I say something here?" he asked after a moment, abandoning his efforts to make the paper magically one piece again.

Melissa nodded grimly, her gaze focused on the desk.

"Maybe it's not my place . . ." he began tentatively.

"That's never stopped you before," Melissa said with the hint of a smile.

"Yeah." He mussed his hair again. "Well, I guess I'm a little confused by what's going on. The thing is, not more than two weeks ago I stood in this very office and listened to you swear on the old alumni files that you'd do anything you had to to get money from Dakin Quarry." He looked from one half of the torn paper to the other, then shook his head. "And now you're tearing up his messages. I'm wondering exactly what it was you meant two weeks ago."

Inside Melissa something snapped like a rubber band.

"You, too?" she exploded, rising to her feet behind the desk. "You think when I said anything I really meant *anything?* You think I ought to jump into bed with him to get his lousy few hundred thousand dollars?"

She glared at Jeff. His face had flushed redder than

his tousled hair, and his eyes were wider than she had ever seen them before. He blinked rapidly.

"Geez, who said anything about *sleeping* with anybody?" he asked plaintively, his voice almost a whisper. "That's . . . I mean, I'm devoted to my job, but that's immoral!"

He stood staring at her, still blinking, and Melissa had the sudden, uncomfortable sensation that he was blinking back tears.

She put both hands flat on the desk and took in a deep breath. "Oh, Jeff . . ." She tried on a smile for size. "Poor Jeff. I'm sorry. I thought you were saying I ought to be in there doing *anything*, like I'd promised I would."

He shook his head vigorously. "Geez, no. In fact," he went on, sounding more controlled, "maybe what I'm saying is just the opposite."

Melissa sank back down in the chair and pressed the tips of her fingers together. She looked up at Jeff. "What do you mean?"

"Well . . ." He glanced quickly around the room, almost as if searching for an escape route. Then, with a deep breath of his own, he folded his arms over his chest.

"Look, boss. Melissa. I try to keep out of what's going on with you outside this office. Really I do. But lately it's been a little hard to escape the fact that Dake Quarry has been out there somewhere." Jeff waved vaguely in the direction of the window, as if Dake might be wandering aimlessly around the central quad.

"The thing is," he went on, "no matter what role the guy's playing in your private life, he's got another one in here." He pointed at the floor of the office. "In your— 'scuse the formality—professional life. I just don't think you ought to let the one get in the way of the other. If Dake Quarry's got money to donate to Ransom, I don't think you should be tearing up his phone messages. That's all."

He held his hands out, palms up, in a gesture of innocence.

Melissa looked down at the desk thoughtfully and shook her head. What an idiot she'd been, she told herself. She'd been so frazzled about keeping her relationship with Dake private, so no one would think it was all part of her job, and now here she was, letting that same relationship walk right into this office and take over.

"Jeffrey, I should talk to you more often," she said. "Thanks."

He shrugged, and the scarlet slowly began to drain from his face. "No charge," he said. "I just didn't like what I was seeing happen to you."

Melissa smiled and shook her head. "Thanks for being concerned," she said. "It's been a real mess. Bob Rudge, among others, seems to think that I should use my ... the fact that I'm a woman to move things along in my job. I'm so offended by that, that I guess when somebody *is* interested in me as a woman I just can't do my job with them. It's some kind of inverse psychology. But it's never happened before." She shook her head. "Not like this, anyway."

Jeff grinned. "Ah-ha! So my suspicions prove true," he said. "Dake Quarry's the man to watch in Melissa Markham's life. Shirley owes me five dollars."

Melissa's mouth fell open. "You made a *bet?*" she cried. "With Shirley at the alumni office?"

Jeff nodded.

"So much for your thoughtful concern." She scowled at him. "And I thought I was being so careful," she added with a sigh. "No wonder Rudge ..."

Then Melissa straightened her shoulders and folded her hands on the desk. "Anyway, you *don't* win, Jeff. That's just the point. Dake is *not* the man in my life anymore. But he *has* offered the college a minimum of a hundred thousand dollars and a maximum of five hundred thousand. I guess I can manage a phone call to try to get it."

Okay, Markham, she told herself as Jeff left the office, your job is to get this man's money—with no strings *attached*. Go to it.

She pulled Dake's file to the center of her desk and opened it. The memo from President Warren still sat on top, with her note scrawled on it about an honorary degree. The bitterness in Dake's voice when he'd spoken about not graduating rang in her ears. With a touch of impatience, she typed out a memo to the president, formally suggesting that Ransom offer Dakin Quarry an honorary bachelor of arts degree.

Maybe that's one path, she told herself resolutely. She slid a copy of the memo into Dake's file and plopped the original into her OUT basket.

Then she picked up the phone and dialed Windflame Runners.

Dake was on the line almost immediately.

"Hello, Dake," Melissa said politely. "What can I do for you today?"

Dake's voice was soft. "Ah, our professional tone," he said. "Mel, I've been doing some thinking. I need to talk to you."

"I'm listening," she answered.

There was a brief silence. "Mel, I don't think we can do this on the phone."

"On the contrary," she said quickly, "I think the phone is about the best place for us to do business. No distractions. Did you want to talk about a donation again? Because I've been thinking about some possible ways the money could be allocated."

"No," he said, more sharply this time, "I don't want to talk about a donation. I want to talk about us."

Now it was Melissa's turn to sit silently for a moment. "Dake, I don't think that's a good idea."

"Listen to me, Melissa Markham. I was doing just fine six months ago. I'd even put money in the bank for your precious college. Then you walked into my life, and it went all haywire."

"Am I supposed to accept the blame for—for everything that's happened to you in the last six months? I don't think that's fair."

"Pretty close," he answered quickly. Then she could

almost hear him settling himself down at the other end of the phone.

"Mel," he said, "you told me last Saturday that you didn't see much difference between me and Bob Rudge. Now, you can only begin to imagine what that did to me. Here was the woman I love, telling me I was just like a man I hate."

Melissa tried to listen to what Dake was saying, but the word *love* echoed over and over in her brain. He said he loved me, she told herself with a little-girl grin. He said he loved me.

"Mel?"

"Hmm?" She shook her head sharply, forcing her attention back to the conversation.

"Mel, we need to talk about this in person. Please." Dake's voice sounded very controlled; there was none of the playful coaxing he had used on other occasions. "I need to see you. I can be at your apartment in an hour."

He said he loved me. "How about my office?"

"Well . . ."

Melissa sighed. "Okay. The apartment. I'll see you there around four."

Dake was standing on the front porch of the old house, stamping his feet against the cold, when Melissa drove up. He had on jeans and his leather flight jacket, and the tips of his ears were red.

"You ought to get some ear muffs," she called as she locked her car. "Been here long?"

He shrugged. "Ten minutes or so. Just get me inside and pour some coffee into me, and I'll be okay."

Melissa opened the front door and led the way up the stairs. She felt vaguely shy, as if all this were somehow brand-new to her. She was intensely conscious of the sound of Dake's footsteps—his long, slender feet encased today in heavy boots—as they echoed on the stairs behind her. Halfway up she caught a toe awkwardly, and Dake supported her back briefly, making sure she had regained her balance. A quiver of electricity shot from the place where his hand had brushed her to someplace just below her belly.

At the top of the stairs, she took his jacket and hung it on one of the wall hooks. The cold leather crackled a little. Dake leaned over and pulled off his boots, depositing them carefully by the wall, under the coats.

"I really thought I'd never see you again," Melissa said softly.

Dake rubbed his hands together. He had on a sky-blue crewneck sweater over a white shirt, and the soft colors enhanced his bronze skin.

"I thought maybe you wouldn't either," he said ruefully. "I was pretty damn mad."

Melissa ducked her head. "Well, so was I. You deserved it."

"I didn't deserve—" he began sharply, then stopped. "I promised myself we wouldn't start," he said. "Not on that part of it. I've been thinking about some of the rest of what you said. You were right, you know. On the basics."

He had followed her into the huge kitchen, its walls lined with hanging dried herbs, and now he watched as she put a pot of water on to boil.

"You remind me of my parents," he said quietly. "The way you hang on to your principles. I admire that. Even when it makes me mad."

Melissa swung her head around to look at him as she fitted the top of the coffee grinder into place. His smile was a little sheepish.

"My parents taught me what was important, Mel. Doing things because they're right. Trusting people. But I'd buried some of that under..." He shrugged. "Whatever. Anyway, you're helping me find it again, Mel. You're a good teacher."

Melissa looked down at the grinder, letting her hair fall forward to cover cheeks now flushed with embarrassment and pleasure. She pushed a button, and the whirring noise of beans being ground filled the air.

"You're so damn principled, you even grind your own coffee," he added with a little chuckle. "Who could ask for anything more?"

Melissa glanced at him. "So do you," she accused him good-naturedly. "I saw the grinder in your kitchen."

He grinned. "Ah. The observant type. Well, then, it's just one more thing we have in common."

Melissa poured hot water through the finely ground beans, then filled two mugs with steaming black coffee. Cups in hand, they headed back to the living room. Dake sat on the couch, pulled off his socks, and carefully propped his bare feet on the low table in front of him.

Melissa curled up in the big chair and cleared her throat. The sight of his graceful, naked feet reminded her suddenly of that very first evening, the night of the dinner at the Art Institute, when she had gone to his hotel room . . .

"Look, Mel," he said after a moment, interrupting her daydreams, "you were starting to tell me the other night what you know about Bob Rudge. How he runs his department."

Melissa felt herself crumple slightly. Not again, she told herself. Oh, please, after all those beautiful things he said, not again.

She nodded. In her mind's eye, she could see those same bare feet, almost copper-colored, against the faint peach of the Palmer House carpet. She ran her tongue over her lips.

"You know as well as I do that I'm not going to give Ransom College any money as long as things like that are going on."

She looked toward the side window and nodded again, feeling a heavy sense of misery settle over her.

"So you can't do your job," he went on. "You can't get my money. And you know as well as I do that you shouldn't be getting anyone else's money either. Not to perpetuate the likes of Bob Rudge."

Melissa's eyes were half-closed; she was seeing how

Dake had looked standing over her, dangling a wineglass. She didn't say anything.

"So you shouldn't be working there at all," he finished.

Melissa's daydream shattered into crystalline shards.

"Not working there?" she repeated, looking at him sharply. "I don't understand."

Dake gave his head an impatient shake. "Quit," he said. "Turn whatever you have about Rudge over to Warren and quit. Warren seems like a perfectly acceptable type; I'm sure he'll figure out how to deal with Rudge."

Melissa looked at him thoughtfully. "Okay," she said. "So I give the information to Warren, and Warren deals with Rudge. Then why would there be any reason for me to leave Ransom? If Rudge is your only objection?"

Dake grinned. The wide smile gave his face a mischievous appeal, taming the wildness of his high cheekbones and deepset eyes.

"Because I have other plans for you," he said softly.

"Other plans?" she repeated. "What other plans?"

"Come live with me."

Melissa stared at him blankly. "Come live with you?"

He nodded, still grinning. "Come live with me and be my love," he said lightly.

"Come live with you." I sound like an echo, she told herself sharply. Then, with a sudden burst of impatience, she pushed herself up out of her chair.

"And do what?" she asked, abruptly annoyed with Dake, annoyed with herself, annoyed with the whole preposterous situation. "Sit around and give you lectures about not doing deals? Play white knight? Be your conscience? I honestly don't think that's a full-time job."

"Not anymore," Dake said. "I hope."

He rose, too, and he stepped around the coffee table to stand in front of her.

"No. Do whatever you like. Just don't do it for Ransom College. You can find plenty of other places eager for your talents."

He put both hands on her shoulders and leaned down to kiss her. Despite her confusion, Melissa could feel stirrings of anticipation and excitement. She closed her eyes.

Dake's lips brushed her cheek. "Mel," he murmured, "I haven't trusted anyone, not really, in a long, long time."

His mouth touched her eyelids, the bridge of her nose, and the moist warmth of it seemed to drive away her doubts. "I love you, Mel," he murmured.

Melissa felt the last of her hesitations melt beneath his words. "I love you, too," she whispered, but her words were inaudible, lost in the pressure of his mouth against hers.

Gently, he led her back through the hallway to the bedroom. Slowly, with the soft, graceful motions of a cat mothering its young, he undressed her and held her close to him, letting his warmth become hers, letting his strength become hers. Melissa responded to his touch with soft noises and caresses, nuzzling the hollow of his throat, rubbing her cheek against his chest. Together they pulled back the down coverlet on the bed.

Dake touched her face with his hand, first the curve of her cheek, then the line of her eyelid. He let his lips trail after his fingers, sealing the tenderness of his touch with a kiss. "You're so beautiful," he said.

His mouth moved downward, along the long arch of her throat, then sought the comforting warmth of her breasts. With light touches of his tongue he brought the liquid heat to her breasts that signaled to her the urgent need her body felt for Dake's presence. She lay still as his lips found the firmness of her belly, then kissed the tender flesh of her inner thighs. She could hear her breathing quicken, but she felt somehow suspended, like a figure in a lavish illustration for a fairy tale. She waited, her body tingling with anticipation.

Then he was beside her again, his breath warm against her hair. His hands glided over her body, over and over again. It would go on, Melissa knew somewhere deep inside herself, for infinity. This moment would have no end, and yet her body would always be waiting, exquisitely waiting, agonizingly short of fulfillment.

She moaned softly, and the sound seemed to change the nature of Dake's movements. Now his hands sought her more urgently. He shifted his weight so that he lay above her, and he came to her slowly, using the languid responses of her own body to pace himself. She trembled and pulled him close.

Then the need for each other overtook them, and the slow movements of his body quickened. He was a tiger, stalking his prey, and now he had seen it, far in the distance, and he was moving faster, always a little faster, staying low and out of sight in the high grass, his eyes never leaving the animal he was hunting.

Melissa laughed aloud: She was the prey, but she knew that her hunter meant her no harm; she knew her fate and wanted it, wanted it as much as the hunter. She teased him with the quick movements of her body, but she kept always just ahead of him, waiting until she was ready. Then she stopped in a clearing, waiting for him, and she felt the astonishing beauty as his powerful body overtook hers with one final, overwhelming leap, twisting gracefully through the air, and he gave himself to her. Inside, somewhere deep in the center of her where nothing had ever touched before, fireworks exploded.

Afterward Melissa rested her head on Dake's arm. Her body felt drained yet energetic; she wanted to lie here forever, and at the same time she wanted to jump up and run a mile. She turned her head and looked at him tenderly.

Dake was staring at the ceiling, one arm behind his head. "You know," he said, breaking the peaceful silence, "I could relocate the plant. In Colorado, maybe. Or someplace that has no memories for either one of us."

Melissa's eyes widened, and she propped herself up on her elbows. "You can't be serious," she said. "You can't just up and move a factory."

He smiled at the ceiling. "Yes, I can," he said coolly. "If that's what I want to do." He turned his head on the pillow so he could look at her and touched the tip of her nose with his lips. "If you'll do it with me."

She breathed deeply and pushed the covers aside, reached for her robe, and wrapped it around herself. Then she sat cross-legged at the end of the bed, facing Dake as he leaned back against the headboard.

"That's a very nice offer," she said sincerely. "But we both know I can't accept."

Dake shook his head. "I don't know anything of the kind," he said.

"Dake, I have a commitment to Ransom College. I took a job six months ago. This fund-raising campaign is barely off the ground. It'll be two more years of hard work to finish the project. And that's just one project. I want to get the endowment back up where it should be, and—"

Dake waved a hand in the air. "Somebody else did it before you. Somebody else can do it again."

"Somebody else did it incompetently!" she sputtered. Then she shook her head firmly, determined not to get sidetracked. "The point is, you're asking me to renege on a commitment I've made, not just to Ransom but to myself. Just like Ransom reneged on you."

Dake scratched his nose with one finger and looked away. He said nothing.

"Anyway," Melissa went on after a moment, "I *like* my job. I like Chicago. I like Ransom. About the only thing I *don't* like is Bob Rudge, and . . ." She shrugged. And maybe he's not long for that place, she finished silently.

Dake was still looking away, his eyes focused on a wall where Melissa had hung her collection of thrift-shop jewelry and scarves. He sat up straight in the bed and crossed his legs under the covers, and Melissa could see him begin to massage his right calf mechanically.

"Does that leg still bother you?" she asked.

Dake looked at her with a smile. "No," he answered with a shake of his head. "But it helps me think. I'm thinking now. I'm thinking about what you're saying."

Melissa stood up and dressed, her back to Dake. He sat quietly in the bed, only his hand moving slowly on his leg.

"You really won't give it up?" he said finally.

Melissa shook her head. "No." She turned to face him. "I wish you could understand. It's so important to me. Leaving Ransom would be denying that a problem exists between us. Running away from something because we can't find a solution. It would hang over us for the rest of..." She waved a hand helplessly in the air. "It would always be there, unresolved," she finished.

"You mean, you aren't interested in Wonderland anymore."

Melissa smiled. "I never was," she said softly. "I think problems are there to be solved. I don't think disappearing down the rabbit hole solves anything."

He nodded slowly. "Well, then, I guess we'd better stay right here and solve it. How about showing me the stuff you have on the athletic department? Maybe we can work from there."

Melissa stared at him. "Are you serious?" she asked. "No revenge? No bitterness? Just solving a problem?"

He shrugged. "Scout's honor," he said. "Because we're more important than anything that happened fifteen years ago."

Melissa sat down on the edge of the bed again. "Okay. But you have a vested interest in all the athletics stuff. I think it should come from a neutral party."

He stopped rubbing his leg. "I'm a businessman, Mel. I can figure out what a budget means. If Rudge has been doing anything illegal—"

Melissa stared at him. "And I can't?" she interrupted sharply. "I can't figure out if a budget is off? I've been running offices and handling mammoth budgets for eight years!"

He ducked his head under the covers and held up a

hand. "Truce! Sorry!" His head appeared again, emerging slowly from beneath the down coverlet. "Come on, Mel. Let me work with you on this. Let me at least see what you've got."

Melissa turned away. Her glance caught on the heavy wool socks, clean now and rolled into a ball, waiting to be returned to Dake. She picked them up and tossed them at his handsome face.

"Okay," she agreed. "Let's go over to the office right now."

Dake took the socks in one hand and seemed to test their weight, like a shotputter. He was grinning. "Good girl," he said.

It was odd, being at the office when no one else was there. It occurred to Melissa that she had worked late before, but Jeff had almost invariably been on hand; and no matter how early she got in, he was always at his desk. Now everything was dark and silent.

She unlocked the door to Jeff's office and flicked on the light, and she noticed with amusement the neatly labeled piles of work arranged on his desk. It was reassuring to have confirmed once again that Jeff, the free spirit, was every bit as compulsive as she was.

Dake pushed open the door to her office. A silvery glow filtered in from the streetlights outside on the central quadrangle. Melissa started to switch on the overhead light, then stopped. Instead, she circled the room once, turning on the three small lamps, producing a softer aura.

Dake watched her, amused. "Don't want to break the enchantment?" he asked.

Melissa made a little face, then sat down in her desk chair and glanced at a handful of pink phone message slips. Dake thumbed idly through the stack of file folders in her PENDING basket.

"Alan McAllister," she murmured to herself. "Sorry I missed him." She made a note on her calendar.

"Hey, here's me," Dake said playfully, holding up the

familiar folder. Melissa glanced at him. "All the inside information?" he asked, his voice light and teasing.

Melissa reached for the folder, but he pulled it away. "Not much of interest," she said with a shrug. "Records of all your arrests as an undergraduate. Lists of your harlots. That sort of thing."

She stood halfway up and reached across the desk, but Dake kept the folder out of reach. He spread it open at one corner of the desk and began turning over pages slowly, back to front.

"Ah, yes," he said, coming to the newspaper article. "The famous panther escapade. Now *that* was fun."

Melissa rolled her eyes and looked back at her messages. She made another note on her calendar, then began poking through the pile of folders herself, looking for the one Jeff had assembled on the athletics department.

"Here we go," she said after a moment. "This is the stuff that—"

"What's this?" Dake interrupted. He had stopped turning pages. He put both hands flat on the desk and leaned over the file, studying it.

"What's what?"

Melissa stood and came around the desk so she could see what he was looking at. A tiny flicker of misgiving ran through her. "Oh, that's a memo from Warren," she said casually, but keeping the lightness in her voice was suddenly an effort. "From way back after the dinner in November. He'd only just discovered what a prime prospect you were."

Dake continued to stare at the paper. "What's this about an honorary degree?" he asked. His voice was quiet and steady, without a trace of emotion as he read aloud the words she had scrawled across the bottom. "Honorary degree as bait."

He looked up at her, his weight still resting on his hands. "Bait," he repeated.

Melissa shook her head. The flicker of misgiving had become a storm; her whole body felt wracked with it.

Just half an hour earlier, it had seemed as if all her dreams were about to come true. Now things seemed to be dissolving, shattering before her very eyes, and there was nothing she could do about it.

"Dake, I wrote that almost a month ago," she said. "Just after you first told me you hadn't graduated. It seemed like a possibility—"

"But not this," he interrupted. He picked up the memo she had typed to Jack Warren just six hours earlier, just before she had dialed Dake's phone number. "This is dated today. And this time you were pretty sure it would work, weren't you? Because I'd told you how much that degree meant to me the last time we were together. In bed."

Melissa continued to shake her head, almost automatically. "Dake, that's not it at all. You *have* to try to understand. When I wrote that note, I figured we were through as . . . as lovers. But I still had a job to do."

His smile was tight and narrow, and his head was tilted back. In the soft light of the lamps, shadows fell across his face, and his high cheekbones gleamed softly bronze. Melissa could hardly see his dark eyes.

"Had a job to do," he repeated. "So what've you been doing, taking notes all along? You just kept pecking away until you found the weak spot, didn't you, Mel? There it was. And all the time I thought you were falling in love with me."

"Dake!" Melissa cried. She took a step toward him and held out her hand, but he seemed not even to see her. She felt shut out, as if a door had closed somewhere ahead of her; the planes of his body seemed sleek, dangerous.

He shook his head slowly, ignoring her cry and her hand. "You wouldn't get Rudge fired for me, because that was unethical. And I believed you. Talk about ethics . . ."

He closed the folder and pushed it back toward the center of the desk, then looked at her. The lines of his face were sharply carved, as if from a block of ice, and his eyes were blank.

"Well, thanks anyway, Mel," he said evenly, "but I'm not interested. You can keep your fancy honorary degree, and you can keep your research files, and you can keep Ransom College. Sorry to say, it just didn't work. The whole damn thing."

Suddenly Melissa felt herself harden in a rush of anger. It wasn't fair! She had tried so hard, so very hard.

"Damn it, Dake," she said aloud, "be fair. Think about what I've been juggling all this time."

"Fair is not a word I've associated with this place in the past," he said coldly. "I was stupid to think I could start now." Then he turned and walked away, out the door.

And out of my life, Melissa thought.

Her throat felt tight, constricted, and she reached up to loosen the scarf she had tied around it with frivolous abandon when she had left her apartment. Her breath was coming in small, choked gasps. She could feel the prickly heat of tears welling in her eyes, and she batted at them with the back of one hand, but it was no use. There were too many. The tears came, and with them sobs that shook her whole body.

"Damn," she said once, quietly.

Then she picked up the thick file on Dakin Quarry and threw it, as hard as she could, against the door he had closed behind himself. The papers made a hissing sound as they slid in a jumble to the rug.

- *10* -

JUST TWO DAYS before Christmas, Melissa decided to drive home for the holidays. Anything, she suspected, would be better than being by herself. And the big, high-spirited family celebration would mask her own unhappiness; no one would even have to notice her troubles.

She dove into the chaos of Marshall Field's for a full day, scurrying from department to department, picking up last-minute gifts to supplement the ones she had sent the week before, and Christmas Eve morning she headed east. It wasn't going to be much of a Christmas no matter where she was, she told herself dryly, but at least it would be noisy at home.

As the flat Indiana countryside slid by, she thought about the manila envelope she had pushed under President Warren's door late the afternoon before. She wondered idly if it had been the right thing to do, passing on her summary of the athletics department file without a personal meeting with the president. But her cover memo had requested a meeting as soon as Warren returned from vacation, and that, Melissa told herself with a sigh, was the best she could do.

Her predictions about the cheerfulness of holidays at home proved accurate. There was a light snow on Christmas Day, and the farm looked its beautiful best. In the loving midst of her sisters and brother and their families, she could almost forget about Dakin Quarry and Robert Rudge.

Nieces and nephews joyfully exploded all around her, tearing open gifts, making a shambles of the orderly process her father always attempted to impose on Christmas morning. It was all so familiar, and it was all so wonderful. It was only in the evening, when her siblings had retreated to their nearby homes and the house was quiet again, that she thought about Dake—thought about his smile, so innocent and caring; thought about the warmth of his touch; thought about the strength of his body next to hers.

No amount of hoopla could make her mother miss the signs of her daughter's desolation. Melissa was only partially successful in fending off her questions, and her father, gruffly sympathetic, wrapped his arms around her and insisted that she stay through the first of the year.

On the second day of the new year, exhausted from the eight-hour drive back and feeling just a little empty inside, Melissa unlocked the downstairs door at 106 Elm. But she felt a twinge of relief as she let herself into the high-ceilinged foyer. Going home had been a nice change, even a respite from the pressures of being at Ransom, but she was glad to be back.

A basketful of Christmas cards sat on the old oak table where the doctor always left her mail when she was away. She picked up the handful of cards and sifted through them quickly.

There was also a package on the table, about the size of a shoebox, wrapped in silver foil and tied with a red ribbon. She looked at it for a moment, her forehead furrowed in a small frown. There was no outside wrapping on the package, and no card; apparently it had been hand delivered. She picked it up and shook it once, then smiled. Dr. Graham, of course. Sweet old Dr. Graham had left her a present.

She tucked the package under her arm, picked up the Christmas cards, and dragged her canvas suitcase and her bag of presents up the stairs.

The apartment was cold. Melissa turned up the thermostat and started a small fire in the fireplace, then dumped most of the contents of her suitcase into the clothes hamper. She retrieved her flannel robe and slippers, changed into them, made herself some hot chocolate, and finally settled onto the couch with the cards and the silver-wrapped package.

She opened and read all the cards before turning to the present. Melissa turned it around and around, hunting for some sign of a label or a card. It was curious, she thought; silver foil wasn't really Dr. Graham's style. Something Victorian would have been more like him, or maybe even wrapping paper covered with Santa Clauses. Finally she pulled the gleaming paper carefully off.

It *was* a shoebox. The stylized Windflame logo was on its lid, and inside was a pair of running shoes— Ransom red and white, with a golden lightning bolt down the side.

Melissa stared at them for a long time. Gently, she touched the smooth leather with her fingertips; it felt cool and soft and strong. She slipped her hand into one shoe and lifted it out of its tissue-paper nest. The white leather seemed to glisten in the firelight.

She held the shoe a moment longer, then put it carefully back into the box and folded the tissue paper back into place. The fire danced and crackled and finally faded a little, and Melissa felt something fade inside herself as well—some small fire that had danced in her unconscious. She reached for the phone almost mechanically and dialed Dake's home number, but no one answered.

There was an ache inside her belly that felt as if it would never go away.

The ache was still there the next day when she made her way to her office across the slush that now covered the campus. Jeff was waiting, as usual, at his desk.

"Yo, boss!" he called brightly as she came through the door. "Good Christmas?"

Melissa nodded. "Hi, Jeff. Yours?" She pulled off her muffler and hung her down jacket on a hook.

"Terrific. Just terrific." Jeff stood up and rubbed his hands together, put them in his pockets, then immediately pulled them out again and folded his arms. Melissa watched him curiously.

"Susan's parents liked me," he said with a silly grin. "Something new in my life."

Melissa managed a smile. "Oh, come on, Jeff, you could charm anybody."

He shook his head vigorously. "Nope. Never happened before. Generally I don't get along with parents."

Melissa laughed as she sifted quickly through the pile of mail on Jeff's desk and pulled out a couple of letters. "So what's going on here?" she asked, moving on toward her own office. "Anything new?"

He trailed after her, a note in his hand. "Yep. Big doings," he said, handing her the paper. "The phone was ringing when I walked in the door this morning."

Melissa glanced at the message.

"Warren?" she said skeptically. "I thought he wasn't supposed to be back on campus for two weeks. He's here? And he wants to see me now?"

Jeff nodded. "That was the word. At nine. Donna sounded kind of grim."

Melissa frowned. "Donna say what it was about?"

"Uh-uh. Nothing. It's all very mysterious."

Melissa looked at him as she settled into the chair behind her desk. "Well, it must be the athletics stuff. I left the summary under Warren's door, and I asked for an appointment as soon as he got back."

She thumbed through the stack of folders that sat on one side of her desk, hesitated, then went back through them again more slowly.

"Jeffrey," she said sharply, looking up, "did you do something with that file? The one you made up on Rudge?"

His eyes widened, and he shook his head. "It was right there in that pile the last time I saw it."

Melissa pushed herself up from the desk. Her stomach felt quivery, on the edge of sick. "It must be here somewhere," she said. "You hunt around out there. It's the only evidence I've got to back up the stuff in that summary."

She went through each pile of folders, one by one, and then through the file cabinet, with no results. A hard lump of fear formed deep inside her. Finally she leaned against the doorjamb between Jeff's office and her own.

"It's gone," she said evenly. "Someone's taken it. Someone's been in here over vacation. Without that file, there's no reason for anyone to believe . . ."

The fear in her stomach turned in on itself and formed a knot, hard and huge. Images appeared in her head: Dake Quarry glancing through his own file, his face grim and taut; Dake offering the college half a million dollars for Rudge's job; then Coach Rudge, red-faced, suggesting that if she reported about his department to the president, he would pass on a report of his own. About how she conducted her fund-raising affairs. She pressed a hand to her belly.

She closed her eyes, and other pictures began to form in her mind: Dake grilling steaks in their log cottage, his cheeks ruddy from the heat; Dake holding her in his arms, telling her he loved her, asking her to come with him; Dake offering to move his plant to another state, just for her.

He hadn't done this, hadn't taken the file; suddenly she knew that as surely as she knew she loved him.

The fear slowly began to dissipate, the knot to untie and dissolve. In its stead came a rush of love for Dake so strong and steady that it threatened to knock her over. She pressed her body against the door for support. She knew it now; nothing Rudge or President Warren or anybody else had to say would change the fact that she loved him. If Rudge had the evidence, so be it. If the president thought she was unethical, so be it.

He's worth it all, she told herself fiercely, and he's worth fighting for. And if they think my conduct has been unbecoming, then they can *have* their damn job.

"I'm going on over there, Jeff," she said, pulling her jacket back off its hook. "See you whenever."

The old stone house that held the president's office was directly across the quadrangle, but Melissa's nose was already frozen by the time she reached the front door. Bob Rudge's beach-ball frame was parked comfortably on a sofa in the president's waiting room. She nodded a terse greeting, and he grinned.

"Mornin', missy. You got the summons, too?" he asked.

She nodded again and looked a little more closely at Rudge. There was a thin line of sweat across his upper lip, and his complexion seemed a little redder than normal. Maybe, she thought abruptly, maybe Rudge *hadn't* taken the file. But if he didn't have it, she didn't want to think about who did.

A buzzer sounded, and the president's secretary picked up her intercom and listened for a moment. Then she stood up.

"You can both go in now," she said with a smile at Melissa that Melissa could only interpret as sympathetic.

Rudge pushed the door open and politely gestured Melissa in ahead of him. Jack Warren stood behind his big wooden desk, a picture-postcard view of the main quadrangle out the window behind him. Melissa saw with surprise that Alan McAllister already occupied one of the big leather chairs in the office.

"Alan," she said, holding out a hand. "How was your trip? Are the girls all right?"

Alan rose and took her hand in both of his. "Very nice, just fine. It was nice to see the kids," he said with a smile that seemed anxious to Melissa, "but it's nice to be back. How about you? Did you go home after all?"

Melissa nodded. She had the uncomfortable sensation that both President Warren and Rudge were watching her closely, and she turned quickly to look at them.

"Dr. Warren," she said, reaching over the desk to shake his hand. "We didn't expect you back on campus for another couple of weeks."

Behind her, Melissa could hear Rudge greeting Alan McAllister with his usual heartiness.

Warren shook his head. "Things came up," he said tersely. "You had a nice holiday?"

"Yes," she answered as casually as she could. "I didn't decide to go home until a couple of days before Christmas. I just got back last night."

Warren was nodding. "That explains why we couldn't get hold of you," he said. His normally booming voice was pitched a little lower than usual.

He waved toward a chair, and Melissa sat down, grateful for the support. She could still feel where the knot in her stomach had been; a sort of vague emptiness was there now. She wanted nothing more than to have this meeting, whatever it was about, over with. Then she would run to the nearest phone and call Dake, and she would explain to him that she loved him, and everything would be all right again.

She chewed on her lower lip. You hope, she told herself flatly. You hope.

The three men followed her lead and sat down.

"Could I ask," she said in a crisp and businesslike tone, "what this is all about?"

The president cleared his throat and swiveled his chair around for a moment so he could look out the big window. Then he turned back and faced the others.

"It has always been my belief," he began formally, "that institutions of higher learning should serve as models in all respects for their students. We must not only provide quality teachers, but everything we do, all our actions, must be absolutely above reproach."

Melissa closed her eyes briefly. So Rudge got to him,

she thought. So Rudge explained I'm sleeping with Dake Quarry as a fund-raising tactic. And Warren believed him. When she opened her eyes again, she looked steadily at the president.

"Even we as administrators," he went on, "must be ethically and morally sound. Not to mention legally."

Melissa blinked. Legally? Surely there was no question of a *legal* problem . . .

Behind her, she heard the door to the president's office open softly. Alan McAllister to her right raised a hand in greeting. She glanced at Rudge. He sat frozen in his seat, and his small eyes were focused on the newcomer; he looked very much, Melissa thought with a sudden twinge of amusement, like the snowman she and Dake had built at Lake Geneva. She smothered a little smile.

Whoever had entered the room stood almost directly behind her; there was no way she could see who it was without twisting entirely around in her chair.

President Warren rose. "Quarry!" he said, booming out his greeting in a more normal tone. "I was afraid we'd have to do without you!"

Melissa angled herself around. Dake stood just inside the door of the office, and Melissa gulped. It was the first time she had ever seen him in a business suit—brown pinstripe, with a fashionably loose jacket that couldn't hide his strong, angular shoulders or the narrowness of his clipped waist. His tie was woven, cream-colored and brown. His cheeks were glowing from the cold, and his dark eyes glittered. He was, she thought, the most beautiful creature she had ever seen.

Melissa took in a deep breath. She could feel her heartbeat quicken, and she rubbed damp palms against her wool skirt. Then she wove her fingers together and pressed her hands into her lap, taming the instinct of her body to leap up and take hold of him, to gather him into her arms and never let him go.

Dake nodded at her. He was smiling, and it was the same remarkable smile she had first seen months before;

it lent his lean and shadowed face the innocence of a small boy.

With a quick nod, Melissa turned back to face President Warren.

"Come on in, Dake, and have a seat. We've really just started."

From the corner of her eye, Melissa saw Dake settle his tall frame into a chair to Rudge's left.

"Let me be a little more specific now," Warren went on. "Just before Christmas, I suddenly got bombarded with urgent messages from people who had to see me immediately. Melissa wanted an appointment about something very important. Mr. McAllister here wanted a meeting as soon as possible. Coach Rudge hinted that he had some vital information for me."

He waved a hand in the air. "As you all know, I *was* planning a vacation in Vermont." Warren's tone was suddenly dry. "So I turned everybody down. But apparently that wasn't quite good enough for anybody but Melissa. Melissa simply put her information in writing and slid it under my door, for me to look at after Christmas. The rest of you . . ."

Melissa glanced around quickly. So the envelope had reached Dr. Warren. But without the backup information in the file, all the charges she had made in her memo were worthless. There was no doubt in her mind that, by this time, the files in Rudge's own office showed no trace of the problems. She tried to steel herself for the moment when Warren would ask her for her evidence.

Warren nodded at Rudge, and the coach shifted his massive body a little. "First of all, there was Bob," the president went on. "Bob attended a luncheon with me in New York, just before the holidays. He managed to whisper something in my ear about some . . . improper behavior on the part of Ms. Markham. Something about the methods she was using in approaching Mr. Quarry."

A touch of red appeared in Warren's cheeks, and he rubbed his hands together nervously. He looked at

Melissa, and the corners of his mouth turned down just a little.

"Now this wasn't something I necessarily accepted at face value," he added quickly, clearly uncomfortable, "although I *had* seen..." He swiveled away again and cleared his throat. "Well, I did inadvertently observe a rather warm exchange once. That day at the football game."

Melissa glanced at Dake, wide-eyed, but he was staring at the president attentively.

"Dr. Warren," she said firmly, "I told you I was having some...difficulty with Mr. Quarry. I told you that before Christmas. That I wanted you to take over."

Warren nodded. "Yes, you did. And I was by then aware of what sort of difficulty it was. Frankly, I would have let the whole thing drop," he went on, still facing the window, "if Mr. Quarry hadn't turned up in New York, too."

Melissa turned to stare at Dake. "New York?" she murmured. Dake glanced at her and smiled, then turned back toward Warren.

The president swiveled his chair back. "In the course of talking with Mr. Quarry about a major donation, I... uh...I raised the question of impropriety." His voice was muted, almost a mumble. "I have been made aware of the existence of an escrow fund. A hundred-thousand-dollar escrow fund, put aside for Ransom last spring— well before Ms. Markham ever set eyes on Mr. Quarry, as I understand it."

Melissa turned sideways and stared at Dake. They had *talked* about it, the two of them—about *her!* She sank down slightly into her chair, still glaring at Dake. Rudge, sitting between them, was even redder than before, and the line of sweat over his lip had been joined by one across his forehead. He glanced at her, and his eyes were almost completely hidden between folds of flesh.

"So of course the whole issue was ridiculous," Warren concluded with a quick smile at Melissa. "But in the meantime, Mr. McAllister had *also* turned up in New York."

The president rolled his eyes. "You can see what was happening to my vacation," he added. "In any case, both Alan and Mr. Quarry, independent of each other, raised some serious charges about the way you run things over there in the fieldhouse, Bob."

Melissa blinked. McAllister? And Dake?

Warren turned his chair slightly so that he was looking directly at Rudge. He put his elbows on the desk and pressed his fingertips together. "Mr. McAllister had been concerned about it for some time, and he felt finally there was an urgent need for some kind of investigation. Mr. Quarry suggested that that investigation had already been at least partly undertaken—by Ms. Markham's office."

Rudge turned toward Melissa and glared, his bright blue eyes suddenly wide. "Now I don't think—" he began.

"Let me finish, Bob. I'm afraid I was very concerned about the seriousness of some of the charges being made. I came back to campus immediately after Christmas." He sighed deeply. "So much for Vermont.

"In any case," he continued, "I came back to find an envelope from Melissa under my office door, containing a cogent summary of some pieces of information her assistant had collected. Some very serious allegations."

He nodded at Melissa, and she felt her bones melt into the cushions of her chair. Here it comes, she told herself with a sigh. Now comes the part where he asks for my evidence.

"I couldn't get hold of you," Warren said in a voice that sounded much too casual to Melissa's hypersensitive ears, "so I took the liberty of having Donna hunt down the folder in your office." He smiled at Melissa. "I'm sorry. No one was around, and we couldn't reach you anywhere."

Melissa felt as if a huge weight had suddenly been lifted from her, and she straightened her shoulders. She shook her head numbly. "I just noticed it was gone," she said.

Alan leaned toward her. "I'd been nosing around all fall, Melissa," he chimed in, "and I had some information, too. But not as much as you." He turned in his chair to look at Rudge. "The only reason Mr. Rudge was permitted to carry on for so long was that the president before Jack had a soft spot for winning teams. But when I started getting really involved in alumni affairs, after Jack arrived . . . well, some of us feel that winning teams don't mean much unless it's being done the right way."

Melissa looked at Alan. "Really, I didn't have anything to do with it," she said weakly. "I just mentioned the possibility. My secretary Jeffrey did it all."

"You pulled it together into a coherent case, Melissa. That's what we needed."

She turned to look at Dake. He had finally shifted his gaze, and now his dark eyes rested squarely on her. Even from a distance, with Rudge between them, she could feel the radiant heat of his gaze brushing her cheek. She smiled tentatively, and he winked.

Suddenly Rudge was on his feet, the heavy flesh of his chins trembling. "I've done nothing illegal," he said, his tone challenging. "Not a thing. You can comb those records from here to kingdom come. I think this young lady has gotten in way over her pretty head."

President Warren rose from his chair, both hands on the desk. "You're right, of course, Bob. As of yet we've found no technical illegalities. But morally and ethically, your actions, your leadership . . ." He shook his head sadly. "We are terminating your contract as of today, Bob."

Rudge's breathing had turned into a steady wheeze. "I've won more games for this place—" he blustered, then stopped.

Warren shook his head. "Winning isn't everything, Bob. As a coach, you should know that better than anyone. You might want to start getting your things organized now."

Rudge's round, rubbery body seemed to deflate as he collapsed briefly back into his chair. Then he pulled himself up to his feet and, with a nod at Warren, another at McAllister, and a quick glare at Melissa, left the room.

"First time I've ever seen him without something to say," Alan muttered.

"Well," Warren said after a moment, "I guess that's that. Thank you all for coming. Melissa, I'm sorry we had to insult you by taking Rudge's insinuations seriously, even for a moment."

The empty space that had replaced the knot in Melissa's stomach was filled with a sense of accomplishment. She grinned at the president.

"No apologies necessary," she said.

"Except from me," Dake's deep voice broke in. "As usual. I am apologizing one more time. God knows, I hope it'll be the last."

"Oh, no," Melissa answered quickly, shaking her head sharply. "You really don't need ... it's ..."

Don't do this, Dake, she silently beseeched. Don't reveal all in front of my boss and the president of the alumni association. Don't make any bigger fool out of me than I've already made out of myself.

Dake grinned at her. "Get my present?" he asked, seemingly oblivious to her discomfiture.

Melissa glanced at the other two men. They were smiling broadly, and she focused her embarrassed gaze on her hands, still resting in her lap. "Not until last night," she muttered. "Thank you. I tried to call, but there wasn't any answer."

"I was in Colorado for Christmas. With my parents." He took hold of the tie and held it out for her inspection. "My mother's taken up weaving," he said easily. "Just like yours."

Melissa glanced up at the tie. "Very nice," she murmured.

Get me out of here, she prayed silently.

"I didn't get in until late last night," Dake went on cheerily. "The shoes were a peace offering. I brought them by on Christmas Eve, but you weren't around."

"A peace offering?" she repeated. She looked up at him, and this time she allowed her gaze to remain on his face. His lean, lovely, wild face.

"Yep."

He rose. He was several inches taller than Jack Warren, and he seemed to fill the office with his strength. He took a step toward the desk and turned, so he could see Melissa clearly.

"I had a bad experience at this college once," he said slowly. "As everyone here knows. The bad things I learned here stayed with me for fifteen years."

He braced a hip against the president's desk. "But over the course of the last few months, since I've renewed my association with Ransom to some degree, I've been very impressed with the new people in charge here. President Warren, Alan..." He waved a hand at the two men, and then at Melissa. "Mel."

Melissa smiled a little hesitantly.

"Especially Mel."

Mel. It struck her once again how much she liked the sound of that nickname.

She lowered her head, knowing that the warmth she felt in her cheeks was painting them red beneath their light wash of freckles, and she picked at a tiny piece of lint on her skirt.

"I'm...sorry the honorary degree business offended you, Dake," she murmured, no longer so self-conscious about the others in the room. "It seemed like a good idea at the time."

"Hey," he said a little impatiently, "this is *my* apology. You can't have it. Anyway, I've thought the whole thing over, and I've decided that I might just *accept* that offer. If it's officially made, of course," he added with a nod at President Warren. "My parents kind of liked the idea."

He grinned at Melissa. "The thing is, Jack's told me *that* Ransom now gives credit for some kinds of life experience, and I'm thinking *that maybe we* could work out a *deal...*"

"A *deal!*" Melissa cried without thinking, pushing herself halfway out of her chair. "Please, Dake, no more deals!"

Suddenly Alan McAllister laughed out loud. She turned to look at him.

"I'm sorry," Alan said, a little breathless from his own merriment. "That just sounded so heartfelt, Melissa—it struck my funnybone. I gather that's a sore subject between you two."

Melissa nodded gravely. But Dake was smothering a smile of his own, and Melissa let the intensity of her response wash away in the face of their amusement, like a sand castle too close to the ocean.

Dake placed a hand on Melissa's shoulder, his thumb just grazing the side of her throat. Her inhibitions dissolved, she tilted her head a little and rubbed her cheek against the back of his hand.

"Anyway," he said, "the fact is, I might not really need another degree." The pressure of his hand strengthened just a little, and Melissa felt a tiny charge of electricity race through her. "I'm very much hoping to add both a B.A. and an M.B.A. to my family real soon."

He leaned to let his lips graze Melissa's hair. She looked happily up at him, then quickly at Alan and Jack Warren. She was fully aware that her cheeks were now blazing red.

"I think that might be arranged," she said softly.

- *Epilogue* -

MELISSA SAT, SIPPING COFFEE, on the stone terrace of the Colorado ski lodge, alternately reading her newspaper and glancing over at Dake. It was a source of immense pleasure to her that after almost a year of marriage her passion for him had not lost an iota of its intensity, while the loving friendship between them had constantly grown. She smiled, savoring the brilliant white sunlight reflected off the mountain.

She lowered her newspaper slightly to watch the early-morning skiers already on the slopes.

"I don't know where those people get their energy," she said with a shake of her head. "I could no more ski before breakfast than fly."

Dake laughed, and the sound of his amusement echoed through the almost silent valley. The only other noise was the soft murmuring of the couples scattered around the huge terrace and the occasional hissing of skis against hard-packed snow.

"Those people probably aren't expecting babies in five months," he said finally.

"Mmm." Melissa nodded thoughtfully and lowered her gaze back to the paper. "Maybe not."

They were quiet for a moment; then she frowned as a small boxed article caught her eye.

"Dake," she said, "did you see the sports section yet?"

He lowered his copy of the *Wall Street Journal* and shook his head. "Something interesting?"

Melissa nodded impatiently. "Would you look at this?" she asked, a note of scorn in her voice as she folded open the paper and handed it to her husband. He read it through, then shook his head slowly.

"So Rudge found himself a job," he said with a smile.

"Not just a job," Melissa responded indignantly. "A job coaching football. In some new professional league." She pulled the newspaper back and glared at the article. "The Denver Coyotes. In the North American Football Conference. Dake, do you think we should do something?" She looked over at her husband.

"Nope," he said. "I'm not a vindictive person." He smiled serenely at Melissa. "You taught me that," he added. Then he reached a hand out and rested it on her shoulder, and his smile broadened. The sun, edging its morning path across the terrace, caught the glimmer of mischief in his dark eyes.

"Besides," he said, "I have it on good authority that the North American Conference won't last out a single season. Alan McAllister knows the commissioner."

He stretched his long legs in front of him. Almost instinctively, Melissa leaned over and began massaging his right calf, making small circles against the hard flesh.

"Ah," he murmured as he leaned his head back against his chair. "How did I ever survive without you?"

Melissa smiled and looked out over the white mountains.

"Heaven knows," she said so softly that she wasn't sure he had even heard.

Second Chance at Love®

____ 0-425-07977-5	BRIEF ENCOUNTER #252 Aimée Duvall	$2.25
____ 0-425-07978-3	FOREVER EDEN #253 Christa Merlin	$2.25
____ 0-425-07979-1	STARDUST MELODY #254 Mary Haskell	$2.25
____ 0-425-07980-5	HEAVEN TO KISS #255 Charlotte Hines	$2.25
____ 0-425-08014-5	AIN'T MISBEHAVING #256 Jeanne Grant	$2.25
____ 0-425-08015-3	PROMISE ME RAINBOWS #257 Joan Lancaster	$2.25
____ 0-425-08016-1	RITES OF PASSION #258 Jacqueline Topaz	$2.25
____ 0-425-08017-X	ONE IN A MILLION #259 Lee Williams	$2.25
____ 0-425-08018-8	HEART OF GOLD #260 Liz Grady	$2.25
____ 0-425-08019-6	AT LONG LAST LOVE #261 Carole Buck	$2.25
____ 0-425-08150-8	EYE OF THE BEHOLDER #262 Kay Robbins	$2.25
____ 0-425-08151-6	GENTLEMAN AT HEART #263 Elissa Curry	$2.25
____ 0-425-08152-4	BY LOVE POSSESSED #264 Linda Barlow	$2.25
____ 0-425-08153-2	WILDFIRE #265 Kelly Adams	$2.25
____ 0-425-08154-0	PASSION'S DANCE #266 Lauren Fox	$2.25
____ 0-425-08155-9	VENETIAN KISS #267 Kate Nevins	$2.25
____ 0-425-08199-0	THE STEELE TRAP #268 Betsy Osborne	$2.25
____ 0-425-08200-8	LOVE PLAY #269 Carole Buck	$2.25
____ 0-425-08201-6	CAN'T SAY NO #270 Jeanne Grant	$2.25
____ 0-425-08202-4	A LITTLE NIGHT MUSIC #271 Lee Williams	$2.25
____ 0-425-08203-2	A BIT OF DARING #272 Mary Haskell	$2.25
____ 0-425-08204-0	THIEF OF HEARTS #273 Jan Mathews	$2.25
____ 0-425-08284-9	MASTER TOUCH #274 Jasmine Craig	$2.25
____ 0-425-08285-7	NIGHT OF A THOUSAND STARS #275 Petra Diamond	$2.25
____ 0-425-08286-5	UNDERCOVER KISSES #276 Laine Allen	$2.25
____ 0-425-08287-3	MAN TROUBLE #277 Elizabeth Henry	$2.25
____ 0-425-08288-1	SUDDENLY THAT SUMMER #278 Jennifer Rose	$2.25
____ 0-425-08289-X	SWEET ENCHANTMENT #279 Diana Mars	$2.25
____ 0-425-08461-2	SUCH ROUGH SPLENDOR #280 Cinda Richards	$2.25
____ 0-425-08462-0	WINDFLAME #281 Sarah Crewe	$2.25
____ 0-425-08463-9	STORM AND STARLIGHT #282 Lauren Fox	$2.25
____ 0-425-08464-7	HEART OF THE HUNTER #283 Liz Grady	$2.25
____ 0-425-08465-5	LUCKY'S WOMAN #284 Delaney Devers	$2.25
____ 0-425-08466-3	PORTRAIT OF A LADY #285 Elizabeth N. Kary	$2.25

Prices may be slightly higher in Canada.

Available at your local bookstore or return this form to:

SECOND CHANCE AT LOVE
Book Mailing Service
P.O. Box 690, Rockville Centre, NY 11571

Please send me the titles checked above. I enclose _____. Include 75¢ for postage and handling if one book is ordered; 25¢ per book for two or more not to exceed $1.75. California, Illinois, New York and Tennessee residents please add sales tax.

NAME_____

ADDRESS_____

CITY_____ STATE/ZIP_____

(allow six weeks for delivery)   SK-41b

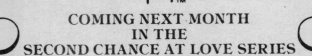

COMING NEXT MONTH
IN THE
SECOND CHANCE AT LOVE SERIES

QUESTIONNAIRE

1. How do you rate _____
   (please print TITLE)
   ☐ excellent   ☐ good
   ☐ very good   ☐ fair   ☐ poor

2. How likely are you to purchase another book
   in this series?
   ☐ definitely would purchase
   ☐ probably would purchase
   ☐ probably would not purchase
   ☐ definitely would not purchase

3. How likely are you to purchase another book by
   this author?
   ☐ definitely would purchase
   ☐ probably would purchase
   ☐ probably would not purchase
   ☐ definitely would not purchase

4. How does this book compare to books in other
   contemporary romance lines?
   ☐ much better
   ☐ better
   ☐ about the same
   ☐ not as good
   ☐ definitely not as good

5. Why did you buy this book? (Check as many as apply)
   ☐ I have read other
       SECOND CHANCE AT LOVE romances
   ☐ friend's recommendation
   ☐ bookseller's recommendation
   ☐ art on the front cover
   ☐ description of the plot on the back cover
   ☐ book review I read
   ☐ other _____
           _____
           _____

(Continued...)

6. Please list your three favorite contemporary romance lines.
_____
_____
_____

7. Please list your favorite authors of contemporary romance lines.
_____
_____
_____
_____
_____
_____
_____

8. How many SECOND CHANCE AT LOVE romances have you read? _____

9. How many series romances like SECOND CHANCE AT LOVE do you <u>read</u> each month? _____

10. How many series romances like SECOND CHANCE AT LOVE do you <u>buy</u> each month? _____

11. Mind telling your age?
☐ under 18
☐ 18 to 30
☐ 31 to 45
☐ over 45

☐ Please check if you'd like to receive our <u>free</u> SECOND CHANCE AT LOVE Newsletter.

We hope you'll share your other ideas about romances with us on an additional sheet and attach it securely to this questionnaire.

• •

Fill in your name and address below:
Name _____
Street Address _____
City _____ State _____ Zip _____

Please return this questionnaire to:
SECOND CHANCE AT LOVE
The Berkley Publishing Group
200 Madison Avenue, New York, New York 10016